A senior trying to set a password

WINDOWS: Please enter your new passw(
USER: cabbage
WINDOWS: Sorry, the password must be more than 8 characters.
USER: boiled cabbage
WINDOWS: Sorry, the password must contain 1 numerical character.
USER: 1 boiled cabbage
WINDOWS: Sorry, the password cannot have blank spaces.
USER: 50bloodyboiledcabbages
WINDOWS: Sorry, the password must contain at least one upper case character.
USER: 50BLOODYboiledcabbages
WINDOWS: Sorry, the password cannot use more than one upper case character consecutively.
USER: 50BloodyBoiledCabbagesShovedUpYourAssIfYouDon'tGiveMeAccessNow!
WINDOWS: Sorry, the password cannot contain punctuation.
USER: ReallyPissedOff50BloodyBoiledCabbagesShovedUpYourAssIfYouDontGiveMeAccessNow
WINDOWS: Sorry, that password is already in use.

Three couples went in to see the minister to see how to become members of his church. The minister said that they would have to go without sex for two weeks and then come back and tell him how it went. The first couple was retired, the second couple was middle-aged and the final couple was newlywed.
Two weeks went by, and the couples returned to the minister. The retired couple said it was no problem at all. The middle-aged couple said it was tough for the first week, but after that, it was no problem. The newlyweds said it was fine until she dropped the can of paint.
"Can of PAINT!" exclaimed the minister.
"Yeah," said the newlywed man. "She dropped the can and when she bent over to pick it up I had to have her right there and then. Lust took over."
The minister just shook his head and said that they were not welcome in the church.
"That's okay," said the man. "We're not welcome in B&Q either."

An Englishman's wife steps up to the tee and, as she bends over to place her ball, a gust of wind blows her skirt up and reveals her lack of underwear.
"Good God, woman! Why aren't you wearing any knickers?" her husband demanded.
"Well, you don't give me enough housekeeping money to afford any."
The Englishman immediately reaches into his pocket and says, "For the sake of decency, here's £50. Go and buy yourself some underwear."

Next, the Irishman's wife bends over to set her ball on the tee. Her skirt also blows up to show that she is wearing no undies.
"Blessed Virgin Mary, woman! You've no knickers. Why not?"
She replies, "I can't afford any on the money you give me."
He reaches into his pocket and says, "For the sake of decency, here's €50. Go and buy yourself some underwear!"

Lastly, the Scotsman's wife bends over. The wind also takes her skirt over her head to reveal that she, too, is naked under it.
"Sweet mudder of Jesus, Stacey! Where the frig are yer drawers?"
She too explains, "You dinna give me enough money ta be able ta affarrd any."
The Scotsman reaches into his pocket and says, "Well, fer the love 'o Jasus, 'for the sake of decency, here's a comb. Tidy yerself up a bit

Two Irish couples decided to swap partners
for the night.
After 3 hours of amazing sex, Paddy says:
"I wonder how the girls are getting on"

Apparently, wine consumption in Australia has dropped alarmingly - they haven't got any openers.

Police have just released details of a new drug craze that is being carried out in Yorkshire nightclubs. Apparently, Yorkshire club goers have started injecting Ecstasy just above their front teeth.
Police say the dangerous practice is called "e by gum"

A Yorkshire man takes his cat to the vet.
Yorkshireman: "Ayup, lad, I need to talk to thee about me cat."
Vet: "Is it a tom?"
Yorkshireman: "Nay, I've browt it with us."

A Yorkshireman's dog dies and as it was a favourite pet he decides to have a gold statue made by a jeweller to remember the dog by.
Yorkshireman: "Can tha mek us a gold statue of yon dog?"
Jeweller: "Do you want it 18 carat?"
Yorkshireman: "No I want it chewin' a bone yer daft bugger!"

Told the wife today,
"My new job is having sex live on stage."
She said, "Are you having me on?"
I replied, "I'll ask, but so far they've all been thin & pretty!"

A woman gets on a bus with her baby. The driver says: "Ugh, that's the ugliest baby I've ever seen."
The woman walks to the rear of the bus and sits down, fuming. She says to a man next to her: "The driver just insulted me." The man says: "You go up there and tell him off. Go on, I'll hold your monkey for you."

This lady walks into her boss's office one day and says,
"Sir, I'd like to file a sexual harassment complaint."
Her boss says, "Well what's your complaint?"
She says, "My co-worker Joe said my hair smelled nice."
The boss says, "That's really not sexual harassment."
The lady counters, "But, Joe's a midget!"

This lady walks into her boss's office one day and says,
"Sir, I'd like to file a sexual harassment complaint."
Her boss says, "Well what's your complaint?"
She says, "My co-worker Joe said my hair smelled nice."
The boss says, "That's really not sexual harassment."
The lady counters, "But, Joe's a midget!"

A little old lady goes to the doctor and says,
"Doctor I have this problem with gas, but it really doesn't bother me too much because they never smell and are always silent.
As a matter of fact, I've farted at least 20 times since I've been here in your office."
The doctor says, "I see, take these pills and come back to see me next week.
The next week the lady goes back to his office. "Doctor," she says,
"I don't know what you gave me, but now my farts, although still silent, stink terribly!"
The doctor says, "Good, Now that we've cleared up your sinuses, let's work on your hearing."

Children are like farts.......
Your own are ok but you can't stand anyone else's!

Male or Female

FREEZER BAGS: They are male, because they hold everything in...but you can
see right through them.

PHOTOCOPIERS: These are female, because once turned off....it takes a while
to warm them up again.
They are an effective reproductive device if the right buttons are pushed...but can also wreak havoc if you push the wrong Buttons.

TYRES: Tyres are male, because they go bald easily and are often over inflated

HOT AIR BALLOONS: Also a male object... Because to get them to go anywhere.....you have to light a fire under their arse.

SPONGES: These are female...because they are soft......squeezable and retain
water.

WEB PAGES:
Female...because they're constantly being looked at and frequently getting
hit on.

TRAINS: Definitely male... Because they always use the same old lines for picking up people.

EGG TIMERS: Egg timers are female because....over time....all the weight
shifts to the bottom.

HAMMERS: Male..... Because in the last 5000 years.....they've hardly changed
at all...and are occasionally handy to have around.

THE REMOTE CONTROL: Female. Ha! You probably thought it would be male...but
consider this: It easily gives a man pleasure, he'd be lost without it...and while he doesn't always know which buttons to push...he just keeps trying

Man rules

these are our rules!

Please note. These are all numbered #1 on purpose!
Men are not mind readers.

Learn to work the toilet seat. You're a big girl. If it's up, put it down. We need it up, you need it down. You don't hear us complaining about you leaving it down.
Crying is blackmail.
Ask for what you want. Let us be clear on this one:
Subtle hints do not work!
Strong hints do not work!
Obvious hints do not work!
Just say it!
Yes and no are perfectly acceptable answers to almost every question.
Come to us with a problem only if you want help solving it. That's what we do. Sympathy is what your girlfriends are for.
Anything we said 6 months ago is inadmissible in an argument. In fact, all comments become null and void after 7 days.
If you think you're fat, you probably are. Don't ask us.
If something we said can be interpreted two ways and one of the ways makes you sad or angry, we meant the other one.
You can either ask us to do something or tell us how you want it done. Not both.
If you already know best how to do it, just do it yourself.
Whenever possible, please say whatever you have to say during commercials.
Christopher Columbus did not need directions and neither do we...
All men see in only 16 colours, like windows default settings.
Peach, for example, is a fruit, not a colour. Pumpkin is also a fruit. We have no idea what mauve is.
If we ask what is wrong and you say 'nothing,' we will act like nothing's wrong. We know you are lying, but it is just not worth the hassle.
If you ask a question you don't want an answer to, expect an answer you don't want to hear..
When we have to go somewhere, absolutely anything you wear is fine...really.
Don't ask us what we're thinking about unless you are prepared to discuss such topics as football or motor sports.
You have enough clothes.
You have too many shoes.
I am in shape. Round is a shape!

This got the whole of Sydney laughing. Read it and you'll see why! Just imagine sitting in traffic on your way to work and hearing this. Many

Sydney folks DID hear this on the FOX FM morning show in Sydney.

The DJs play a game where they award winners great prizes. The game is called 'Mate Match'. The DJs call someone at work and ask if they are married or seriously involved ...with someone. If the contestant answers 'yes', he or she is then asked 3 random yet highly personal questions.

The person is also asked to divulge the name of their partner with (phone number) for verification. If their partner answers those same three questions correctly, they both win the prize.

One particular game, however, several months ago made the Harbour City drop to its knees with laughter and is possibly the funniest thing you've heard yet.

Anyway, here's how it all went down:

DJ: 'Hey! This is Ed on FOX-FM. Have you ever heard of 'Mate Match'?'
Contestant: (laughing) 'Yes, I have.'
DJ: 'Great! Then you know we're giving away a trip to the Gold Coast if you win.
What is your name? First only please.'
Contestant: 'Brian.'
DJ: 'Brian, are you married or what?'
Brian: (laughing nervously) 'Yes, I am married.'
DJ: 'Thank you. Now, what is your wife's name? First only please.'
Brian: 'Sara.'
DJ: 'Is Sara at work, Brian?'
Brian: 'She is gonna kill me.'
DJ: 'Stay with me here, Brian! Is she at work?'
Brian: (laughing) 'Yes, she's at work.'
DJ: 'Okay, first question - when was the last time you had sex?'
Brian: 'About 8 o'clock this morning.'
DJ: 'Atta boy, Brian.'
Brian: (laughing sheepishly) 'Well...'
DJ: 'Question #2 - How long did it last?'
Brian: 'About 10 minutes.'
DJ: 'Wow! You really want that trip, huh? No one would ever have said that if a trip wasn't at stake.'
Brian: 'Yeah, that trip sure would be nice.'
DJ: 'Okay. Final question. Where did you have sex at 8 o'clock this morning?
Brian: (laughing hard) 'I, ummm, I, well...'

DJ: 'This sounds good, Brian. Where was it at?'
Brian: 'Not that it was all that great, but her mum is staying with us for couple of weeks...'
DJ: 'Uh huh...'
Brian: '...and the Mother-In-Law was in the shower at the time.'
DJ: 'Atta boy, Brian.'
Brian: 'On the kitchen table.'
DJ: 'Not that great?? That is more adventure than the previous hundred times I've done it.
Okay folks, I will put Brian on hold, get his wife's work number and call her up.
You listen to this.'

[3 minutes of commercials follow.

DJ: 'Okay audience; let's call Sarah, shall we?' (Touch tones.....ringing....)
Clerk: 'Kinkos.'
DJ: 'Hey, is Sarah around there somewhere?'
Clerk: 'This is she.'
DJ: 'Sarah, this is Ed with FOX-FM. We are live on the air right now and I've been talking with Brian for a couple of hours now.'
Sarah: (laughing) 'A couple of hours?'
DJ: 'Well, a while now. He is on the line with us. Brian knows not to give any answers away or you'll lose. Sooooooo... do you know the rules of 'Mate Match'?'
Sarah: 'No.'
DJ: 'Good!'
Brian: (laughing)
Sarah: (laughing) 'Brian, what the hell are you up to?'
Brian: (laughing) 'Just answer his questions honestly, okay? Be completely honest.'
DJ: 'Yeah yeah yeah. Sure. Now, I will ask you 3 questions, Sarah. If your answers match Brian's answers, then the both of you will be off to the Gold Coast for 5 days on us.
Sarah: (laughing) 'Yes.'
DJ: 'Alright. When did you last have sex, Sarah?'
Sarah: 'Oh God, Brian....uh, this morning before Brian went to work.'
DJ: 'What time?'
Sarah: 'Around 8 this morning.'
DJ: 'Very good. Next question. How long did it last?'
Sarah: '12, 15 minutes maybe.'
DJ: 'Hmmmm. That's close enough. I am sure she is trying to protect is

manhood. We've got one last question, Sarah. You are one question away from a trip to the Gold Coast. Are you ready?'
Sarah: (laughing) 'Yes.'
DJ: 'Where did you have it?'
Sarah: 'OH MY GOD, BRIAN!! You didn't tell them that did you?'
Brian: 'Just tell him, honey.'
DJ: 'What is bothering you so much, Sarah?'
Sarah: 'Well...'
DJ: Come on Sarah.....where did you have it?
Sarah: 'Up the arse.....'

Bloke from Barnsley with piles asks chemist "Nah then lad, does tha sell arse cream?"
Chemist replies "Aye, Magnum or Cornetto?"

Woman: Do you drink beer?
Man: Yes
Woman: How many beers a day?
Man: Usually about 3
Woman: How much do you pay per beer?
Man: £5.00 which includes a tip
Woman: And how long have you been drinking?
Man: About 20 years, I suppose
Woman: So a beer costs £5 and you have 3 beers a day which puts your spending
each month at £450. In one year, it would be approximately £5400...correct?
Man: Correct

Woman: If in 1 year you spend $5400, not accounting for inflation, the past

20 years puts your spending at $108,000, correct?
Man: Correct
Woman: Do you know that if you didn't drink so much beer, that money could
have been put in a step-up interest savings account and after accounting for compound interest for the past 20 years, you could have now bought a Ferrari?

Man: Do you drink beer?
Woman: No

Man: Where's your Ferrari?

The Third 'Nile' virus is coming!
I thought you would want to know about this e-mail virus.
Even the most advanced Antivirus programs cannot take care of this one.
It appears to affect those who were born prior to 1965.

Symptoms:

1. causes you to send the same e-mail twice.

2. Causes you to send a blank e-mail!

3. Causes you to send e-mail to the wrong person. Yep!

4. Causes you to send it back to the person who sent it to you.

5. Causes you to forget to attach the attachment.

6. Causes you to hit "SEND" before you've finished.

7. Causes you to hit "DELETE" instead of "SEND."

8. Causes you to hit "SEND" when you should "DELETE."

IT IS CALLED THE "C-NILE VIRUS."

A prisoner in jail received a letter from his wife:
"I have decided to plant some vegetables in the back garden. When is the best time to plant them?"
The prisoner, knowing that the prison guards read all mail, replied in a letter:
"Dear wife, whatever you do, do not touch the back garden. That is where I hid all the money."
A week or so later, he received another letter from his wife:
"You won't believe what happened. Some men came with shovels to the house and dug up all the back garden."
The prisoner wrote another letter:
"Dear wife, now is the best time to plant the vegetables.

Two great white sharks swimming in the ocean spied survivors of a sunken ship.
"Follow me son" the father shark said to the son shark and they swam towards the mass of people.
"First we swim around them a few times, with just the tip of our fins showing."
And they did.
"Well done, son! Now we swim around them a few times, with all of our fins showing."
And they did.
"Now we eat everybody!"
And they did.
When they were both gorged, the son asked, "Dad, why didn't we just eat them all in the first place?"
"Why did we swim around and around them?"
His wise father replied,
"Because they taste better if you scare the shit out of them first!"

Suarez won't be joining Arsenal after failing his medical. He suffered a massive asthma attack after breathing in the dust in the Emirates trophy room.

ATTORNEY: What was the first thing your husband said to you that morning?

WITNESS: He said, 'Where am I, Cathy?'
ATTORNEY: And why did that upset you?
WITNESS: My name is Susan!

ATTORNEY: What gear were you in at the moment of the impact?
WITNESS: Gucci sweats and Reeboks.

ATTORNEY: Are you sexually active?
WITNESS: No, I just lie there.

ATTORNEY: What is your date of birth?
WITNESS: July 18th.
ATTORNEY: What year?
WITNESS: Every year.

ATTORNEY: How old is your son, the one living with you?
WITNESS: Thirty-eight or thirty-five, I can't remember which.
ATTORNEY: How long has he lived with you?
WITNESS: Forty-five years.

ATTORNEY: This myasthenia gravis, does it affect your memory at all?
WITNESS: Yes.
ATTORNEY: And in what ways does it affect your memory?
WITNESS: I forget.
ATTORNEY: You forget? Can you give us an example of something you forgot?

ATTORNEY: Now doctor, isn't it true that when a person dies in his sleep, he doesn't know about it until the next morning?
WITNESS: Did you actually pass the bar exam?

ATTORNEY: The youngest son, the 20-year-old, how old is he?
WITNESS: He's 20, much like your IQ.

ATTORNEY: Were you present when your picture was taken?
WITNESS: Are you shitting me?

ATTORNEY: So the date of conception (of the baby) was August 8th?
WITNESS: Yes.
ATTORNEY: And what were you doing at that time?
WITNESS: Getting laid

ATTORNEY: She had three children , right?

WITNESS: Yes.
ATTORNEY: How many were boys?
WITNESS: None.
ATTORNEY: Were there any girls?
WITNESS: Your Honor, I think I need a different attorney. Can I get a new attorney?

ATTORNEY: How was your first marriage terminated?
WITNESS: By death..
ATTORNEY: And by whose death was it terminated?
WITNESS: Take a guess.

ATTORNEY: Can you describe the individual?
WITNESS: He was about medium height and had a beard
ATTORNEY: Was this a male or a female?
WITNESS: Unless the Circus was in town I'm going with male.

ATTORNEY: Is your appearance here this morning pursuant to a deposition notice which I sent to your attorney?
WITNESS: No, this is how I dress when I go to work.

ATTORNEY: Doctor, how many of your autopsies have you performed on dead people?
WITNESS: All of them. The live ones put up too much of a fight.

ATTORNEY: ALL your responses MUST be oral, OK? What school did you go to?
WITNESS: Oral...

ATTORNEY: Do you recall the time that you examined the body?
WITNESS: The autopsy started around 8:30 PM
ATTORNEY: And Mr. Denton was dead at the time?
WITNESS: If not, he was by the time I finished.

ATTORNEY: Are you qualified to give a urine sample?
WITNESS: Are you qualified to ask that question?

ATTORNEY: Doctor, before you performed the autopsy, did you check for a pulse?

WITNESS: No.
ATTORNEY: Did you check for blood pressure?
WITNESS: No.
ATTORNEY: Did you check for breathing?
WITNESS: No.
ATTORNEY: So, then it is possible that the patient was alive when you began the autopsy?
WITNESS: No.
ATTORNEY: How can you be so sure, Doctor?
WITNESS: Because his brain was sitting on my desk in a jar.
ATTORNEY: I see, but could the patient have still been alive, nevertheless?
WITNESS: Yes, it is possible that he could have been alive and practicing law.

Five Englishmen in an Audi Quattro arrived at an Irish border checkpoint. Paddy the officer stops them and tells them: "It is illegal to put 5 people in a Quattro, Quattro means four"
"Quattro is just the name of the automobile," the Englishman retorts disbelievingly.
"Look at the papers: this car is designed to carry five persons."

"You cannot pull that one on me," replies Paddy "Quattro means four.-You have five
people in your car and you are therefore breaking the law".

"The Englishmen replies angrily, "You idiot! Call your supervisor over. I want to speak to someone with more intelligence!"

"Sorry,"
responds Paddy, "Murphy is busy with 2 guys in a Fiat Uno."

Picture the scene. A crowded Court Room being ruled over by a Judge whom over the years had several run ins with a particular court usher. This usher who was retiring the following day was serving his last day in the said Judges courtroom. The Judge was hearing a case where a man had been arrested for using foul and abusive language directed at a

Police Constable mainly using the word "fucker" when confronting the Officer. The Judge threw the Constables case out stating that the word "fucker" could not be construed as being either foul or abusive as it is now used frequently in everyday life. The Court was adjourned for 10 minutes and when the Judge returned the usher called out "please all stand for the fucker wearing the wig" Wasn't really a lot the Judge could do.........

Four Catholic men and a Catholic woman were having coffee. The first Catholic man tells his friends, "My son is a priest, when he walks into a room, and everyone calls him 'Father'." The second Catholic man chirps, "My son is a Bishop. When he walks into a room people call him 'Your Grace'." The third Catholic gent says, "My son is a Cardinal. When he enters a room everyone says 'Your Eminence'." The fourth Catholic man then says, "My son is the Pope. When he walks into a room people call him 'Your Holiness'." Since the lone Catholic woman was sipping her coffee in silence, the four men give her a subtle, "Well....?" She proudly replies, "I have a daughter, slim, tall, 38D breast, 24" waist and 34" hips and the face of an Angel.

When she walks into a room, people say, "Oh My God."

A beautiful, voluptuous blonde haired woman went to a gynaecologist. The doctor took one look at this woman and all his professionalism went out the window.
He immediately told her to undress. After she had disrobed the doctor began to stroke her thigh.
Doing so, he asked her, "Do you know what I'm doing?"
"Yes," she replied, "you're checking for any abrasions or dermatological abnormalities."
"That is right," said the doctor. He then began to fondle her breasts.
"Do you know what I'm doing now?" he asked.
"Yes," the woman said, "you're checking for any lumps or breast cancer."
"Correct," replied the shady doctor.
Finally, he mounted his patient and started having sexual intercourse with her.
He asked, "Do you know what I'm doing now?"

"Yes," she said. "You're catching herpes;
because that's why I came here to see you in the first place."

A Travel Agent had had a very profitable summer and seeing an elderly man and woman looking wistfully at the adverts in his window, he decided to offer them a free holiday. He asked them in and said that he would pay for a holiday in the South of France, 5 star hotel and plane tickets, everything paid for. A few weeks later the elderly lady came into the agency and thanked the Agent profusely and said 'I've just got one question, who was that old bugger I had to share a room with'.

Two Texans were out on the range talking about their favourite sex positions. One said, "I think I enjoy the Rodeo position the best."
"I don't think I have ever heard of that one," said the other cowboy. "What is it?"
"Well, it's where you get your wife down on all fours and then mount her from behind. Then you reach around and cup each one of her breasts in your hands and whisper in her ear, 'These feel just like your sister's."

Then you try and stay on for 8 seconds....

So I've made a pack of cards, deal with it.

2 spring rolls +2 spring rolls = 5 spring rolls, Dim sum

Finally went to Poundland, worst theme park I've ever visited.

Took my wife for a Chinese meal last night, she's never eaten Chinese

before so I asked the waiter what he thought she would like, he replied "I bling house speciarity"
He returned 20 minutes later & put a large pot on the table, he told us not to touch it as it was still very hot.
After about five minutes my wife was just about to lift the lid when she let out a scream, "what's up?" I asked
" the lid just lifted & a pair of eyes were looking at me"
"Ah, he's brought you the Peking duck"

This is a story about a couple who had been happily married for years, the only friction in their marriage was the husband's habit of farting loudly every morning when he awoke the noise would wake his wife and the smell would make her eyes water and make her gasp for air.

Every morning she would plead with him to stop ripping them off because it was making her sick. He told her he couldn't stop it and that it was perfectly natural. She told him to see a doctor, she was concerned that one day he would blow his guts out.

The years went by and he continued to rip them out. Then one Christmas day morning, as she was preparing the turkey for dinner and he was upstairs sound asleep, she looked at the innards, neck, gizzard, liver and all the spare parts, and a malicious thought came to her.

She took the bowl and went upstairs where her husband was sound asleep and, gently pulling the bed covers back, she pulled back the elastic waistband of his underpants and emptied the bowl of turkey guts into his shorts.

Sometime later she heard her husband waken with his usual trumpeting which was followed by a blood curdling scream and the sound of frantic footsteps as he ran into the bath room. The wife could hardly control herself as she rolled on the floor laughing, tears in her eyes! After years of torture she reckoned she had got him back pretty good.

About twenty minutes later, her husband came downstairs in his blood stained underpants with a look of horror on his face. She bit her lip as she asked him what was the matter.

He said, "Honey you were right... all these years you have warned me and

I didn't listen to you." "What do you mean?" asked his wife. "Well, you always told me that one day I would end up farting my guts out, and today it finally happened, but by the grace of god, some Vaseline and two fingers. I think I got most of them back in."

There's a nice offer on Amazon at the moment - if you buy all of Adam & The Ants sheet music, they'll throw in a stand & deliver.

Bought five litres of tippex, big mistake.

You're the guy who invented tippex, correct me if I'm wrong.

The train was quite crowded, and a U. S. Marine walked the entire length looking for a seat, but the only seat left was taken by a well-dressed, middle-aged, French woman's poodle.
The war-weary Marine asked, 'Ma'am, may I have that seat?'
The French woman just sniffed and said to no one in particular 'Americans are so rude. My little Fifi is using that seat.'
the Marine walked the entire train again, but the only seat left was under the yapping dog.
'Please, ma'am. May I sit down? I'm very tired.'
She snorted, 'Not only are you Americans rude, you are also arrogant!'
This time the Marine didn't say a word; he just picked up the little dog, tossed it out the train window, and sat down.
The woman shrieked, 'Someone must defend my honour! This American should be put in his place!'
An English gentleman sitting nearby spoke up, 'Sir, you Americans seem to have a penchant for doing the wrong thing. You hold the fork in the wrong hand. You drive your cars on the wrong side of the road. And now, sir, you seem to have thrown the wrong bitch out the window.

A blonde is sitting at the bar when a stranger asks if she'd like a drink, "yes" she replies, thanking him. They sit and chat for a while and the guy asks if she'd like to go for a drive in his car to which she agrees. The two walk to his car parked in a dark corner of the pubs car park and the blonde climbs into the passenger seat beside him. Just as he's about to start the car he has an urge to kiss her, which he does. To his delight she responds. Seizing the moment he asks her if she would like to get into the back seat, "no" she says, so he carries on kissing her. Things get a little hotter and he asks her again "would you like to get into the back?" "No" she replies again and they carry on canoodling. Things now have become so hot and steamy the guy breaks off and asks again "are you sure you don't want to get in the back?" "I said no didn't I" she retorted, "hell why not?" he asked..... "Because I want to stay in the front with you......"

The British guy lives near Le Bugue in the Dordogne and at the time he was stopped he was as pissed as a fart...
The gendarme signals to him to wind down the window then asks him if he has been drinking, and with a slurring speech the British guy replies; 'Yes, this morning I was at my (hic)..daughter's wedding, and as I don't like church much I went to the cafe opposite and had several beers.'
'Then during the wedding banquet I seem to remember downing three great bottles of wine; (hic)... a corbieres, a Minervois and (hic)...a Faugeres.'
'Then to finish off during the celebrations.... and (hic) during the evening ...me and my mate downed two bottles of Johnny Walker's black label.'
Getting impatient the gendarme warns him; 'Do you understand I'm a policeman and have stopped you for an alcohol test'?
The Brit, with a grin on his face, replies; 'Do you understand that I'm British, like my car, which is right-hand-drive, and that my wife is actually sitting in the other seat, which is the one behind the steering wheel?'

Checking out at Tesco, the young cashier suggested to the older woman that she should bring her own grocery bags because plastic bags weren't good for the environment.

The woman apologised and explained, "We didn't have this green thing back in my earlier days."

The assistant responded, "That's our problem today. Your generation did not care enough to save our environment for future generations."

She was right -- our generation didn't have the green thing in its day. Back then, we returned milk bottles, soft drink bottles and beer bottles to the shop. The shop sent them back to the plant to be washed, sterilised and refilled, so it could use the same bottles over and over. So they really were recycled. But we didn't have the green thing back in our day.

We walked up stairs because we didn't have a lift or escalator in every shop and office building. We walked to the grocers and didn't climb into a 200-horsepower machine every time we had to go two streets. But she was right. We didn't have the green thing in our day.

Back then, we washed the baby's nappies because we didn't have the throw-away kind. We dried clothes on a line, not in an energy gobbling machine burning up 2000 watts -- wind and solar power really did dry our clothes back then. Kids got hand-me-down clothes from their brothers or sisters, not always brand-new clothing. But that young lady is right. We didn't have the green thing back in our day.

Back then, we had one TV or radio in the house -- not a TV in every room. And the TV had a small screen the size of a handkerchief not a screen the size of Yorkshire. In the kitchen, we blended and stirred by hand because we didn't have electric machines to do everything for us. When we packaged a fragile item to send in the post, we used wadded up old newspapers to cushion it, not Styrofoam or plastic bubble wrap.

Back then, we didn't fire up an engine and burn petrol just to cut the lawn. We used a push mower that ran on human power. We exercised by working so we didn't need to go to a health club to run on treadmills that operate on electricity. But she's right. We didn't have the green thing back then.

When we were thirsty we drank from a tap instead of drinking from a plastic bottle of water shipped from the other side of the world. We refilled writing pens with ink instead of buying a new pen, and we replaced the blades in a razor instead of throwing away the whole razor when the blade got dull. But we didn't have the green thing back then.

Back then, people took the bus and kids rode their bikes to school or walked instead of turning their mums into a 24-hour taxi service. We had one electrical socket in a room, not an entire bank of sockets to power a dozen appliances. And we didn't need a computerized gadget to receive a signal beamed from satellites 2,000 miles out in space in order to find the nearest fish and chip shop.

But isn't it sad the current generation laments how wasteful we old folks were just because we didn't have the green thing back then?

To see what all the fuss was about I decided to read Sir Alex Ferguson's autobiography, it's taking me ages though, every time I think I've finished it another 9 pages appear.

Several men are in the locker room of a golf club when a cell phone on a bench rings, a man engages the hands-free speaker function and begins to talk....

MAN: "Hello"
WOMAN: "Honey, it's me. Are you at the club?"
MAN: "Yes."
WOMAN: I am at the mall and found a beautiful leather coat. It's $1,000. Can I buy it?"
MAN: "OK, go ahead if you like it that much."
WOMAN: I also stopped by the Mercedes dealership and saw the new 2014 models. I saw one I really liked."
MAN: How much?"
WOMAN: $60,000.
MAN: "For that price I want it with all the options."
WOMAN: "Great! One more thing. ... The house we wanted last year is back on the market. They're only asking $450,000."
MAN: "Well, then go ahead and buy it but just offer $420,000."
WOMAN: "OK. I'll see you later! I love you!"
MAN: "Bye, I love you too."
The man hangs up. The other men are looking at him in astonishment

Then he asks:
"Anyone know who this phone belongs to?"

After discovering over 200 crows dead on roadsides in Manchester the wildlife trust commissioned an investigation to discover the cause.
Early investigations ruled out the suspected deadly avian flu but further studies revealed that all the crows had been struck by traffic.
Cameras with audio capabilities were set up in nearby trees & on street lamps, this revealed that 98% of the crows were killed by trucks with the other 2% hit by vans & motorbikes, amazingly none were the victims of cars.

Further studies revealed that whenever crows were feeding on roadkill a solitary crow was positioned high up as a lookout.

On listening to the audio recordings they discovered that crows could only say "cah" & not "truck, van or motorbike"

Paddy says to Mick....... "I can't remember the name of that historical Greek film that Brad Pitt was in?"
"Troy" said Mick.
Paddy replied "I feckin' am, but I still can't remember!"

HUMAN RESOURCE PERSON: What would you say is your main weakness?
ELDERLY MAN: Honesty.
HUMAN RESOURCE PERSON: Honesty? I don't think that's a weakness.
ELDERLY MAN: I don't give a shit what you think.

Three young lads talking at school, the first, Jack says I bet you two my Dad is faster than your Dads, the second lad says why what does your Dad do, Jack says his Dad works in a circus and catch's a bullet fired from a gun in his teeth, and that's fast. The second lad Danny says my Dad is an athlete, and can run the 100m faster than Usain Bolt, and that's fast. The third lad Billy says my Dad is faster than both your Dads. How come say the other two. Well says Billy my Dad works for the council. Both Jack and Danny look at each other and say to Billy, how does that make him fast? Billy says he doesn't finish work until 5 o'clock but he's at home by 3.

Got my Liverpool Advent Calendar last week. Went to open my first window this morning and found it was boarded up.

Daddy, how was I born?

A little boy goes to his father & asks ....
"Daddy, how was I born?"
The father answers:
"Well son, I guess one day
you will need to find out anyway!"
Your Mum and I first got together
in a chat room on Yahoo.
Then I set up a date
via e-mail with your Mum
SO we met at a cyber-cafe.
We found a secluded room & disappeared into it
for a short time then we googled each other.
There your mother agreed to a
download from my HARD drive.
Then as soon as I was uploading,
we discovered that neither one of us
had used a firewall, & since it was
too late to hit the delete button,
nine months later a little
Pop-Up appeared that said:
You got Male!

Old guy goes to the Doctor, "Doc, I've got a very embarrassing problem"
"What is it?" The Doctor asks
"Well since I retired my penis has turned a funny shade of orange"
"Hmm" says the Doctor, "that is odd, have you taken up any hobbies that may involve the use of chemicals?"
"No" replies the guy, I just sit watching porn films & eating Wotsits"

A genealogist was doing family history research for Donald Trump. He found out that Trump's mother had been to the doctor to see about an abortion. The doctor said 'you've left it a bit late Mrs Trump, Donald's just started school hasn't he.'

Last night I reached for my liquid viagra and accidently swigged from a bottle of Tippex. I woke this morning with a huge correction.

I was at work yesterday when a female colleague asked me what my ring tone was. I said "light brown like everyone else's". Women are certainly much more forward these days.

The wife suggested I get myself one of those penis enlargers....... so I did....she's 21 and her name's Lucy

My girlfriend said she was leaving me due to my obsession with the 60's group The Monkees. I thought she was joking........And then I saw her face

Yoko Ono has been signed up for the next series of 'I'm a celebrity, get me out of here!' Show bosses think she will do really well since she's been living off a dead beetle for the last thirty years.

What is nasal sex? Fuck nose.

I got sacked last night from the Salvation Army soup kitchen, ungrateful bleeders, all I said was, 'Hurry up for fucks sake, some of us have got homes to go to!'

Christmas is like any other day for me, sitting at the table with a big fat bird that doesn't gobble anymore.

Women should be like golf caddies, either holding your balls or getting your bloody tee ready!

Last night I was sitting watching TV when I heard my wife's voice from the kitchen, 'what you like for dinner my love, chicken, beef or lamb?'
I said, 'Thank you, I'll have chicken please'
She replied, 'You're having soup you fat bastard. I was talking to the cat!'

Not every flower can say love, but a rose can.
Not every flower can survive thirst, but a cactus can.
Not every vegetable can read, but my goodness, look at you having a go!

Got myself a new Jack Russell puppy. He's mainly black and brown with a small white patch, so I've named him Birmingham.

In an Indian restaurant last night having a meal, waiter came over and says, 'Curry Ok?'
I said, 'Go on then, but just one song then fuck off'

I was sat in a restaurant and got hit on the back of the head by a prawn cocktail. I looked round and this bloke shouts, 'That's just for starters!'

Two Irish builders (Patrick and Seamus) are seated either side of a table in a pub when a very smart, well-dressed man enters, orders a beer and sits on a stool at the bar.
The two builders start to speculate about the occupation of the suit

PAT: - I reckon he's an accountant.
SEAMUS: - No way - he's a stockbroker.
Pat: - He ain't no stockbroker! A stockbroker wouldn't come in here!
The argument repeats itself for some time until the volume of beer gets the better of Pat and he makes for the toilet. On entering the toilet he

sees that the suit is standing at a urinal, curiosity and the several beers get the better of him.
Pat: - 'Scuse me.... no offence meant, but me and me mate were wondering what you do for a living?
SUIT: - No offence taken! I'm a Logical Scientist by profession
PAT: - Oh? What's that then?
SUIT: - I'll try to explain by example..... Do you have a goldfish at home?
PAT: - Er ... mmm .... well yeah, I do as it happens!
SUIT: - Well, it's logical that you keep it either in a bowl or in a pond. Which is it?
PAT: - It's in a pond!
SUIT: - Well it's reasonable to suppose that you have a large garden then?
PAT: - As it happens, yes I have got a big garden.
SUIT: - Well then it's logical to assume that, in this town, if you have a large garden then you have a large house?
PAT: - As it happens I've got a five bedroom house .... built it myself!
SUIT: - Well given that you've built a five bedroom house it's logical to assume that you haven't built it just for yourself and that you are quite probably married? And with a family?
PAT: - Yes I am married, I live with my wife and four children.
SUIT: - Well then it is logical to assume that you are sexually active with your wife on a regular basis?
Pat: - Yep! Five times a week!
SUIT: - Well then it is logical to suggest that you don't masturbate very often?
PAT: - Do what? Not me, mate!
SUIT: - Well there you are! That's logical science at work!
PAT: - How's that then?
SUIT: - Well from finding out that you had a goldfish, I've told you about your sex life!
PAT: - I see! That's pretty impressive. Thanks mate!

Both leave the toilet and Pat returns to his mate.

SEAMUS: - I see the suit was in there. Did you ask him what he does?
PAT: - Yep! He's a logical scientist!
SEAMUS: - What's that then?
PAT: - I'll try and explain. Do you have a goldfish?
SEAMUS: - Nope
PAT: - Well then, you're a wanker....

Just seen a dyslexic Yorkshireman wearing a cat flap

There was two old guys in Manchester and they saw a notice outside a pub which read "OAP,s 20 pence a drink" they decide to check it out and ordered 2 pints of beer and the Landlord said, "that will be 40 pence gentlemen" shocked and pleased they handed over the money. After drinking their beer, they go back to get 2 more pints and they ask the Landlord what's going on? He replied he had won £55 million pounds on the Lottery and wanted to give something back to the community. The two old guys thanked him, but asked why the 3 old gents stood at the end of the bar weren't drinking at all. The Landlord replied, "They are from Yorkshire and they are waiting for Happy Hour"

A frog goes into a bank and approaches the teller. He can see from her badge that her name is Patricia Whack.

"Miss Whack, I'd like to get a £30,000 loan to take a holiday."

Patty looks at the frog in disbelief and asks his name. The frog says his name is Kermit Jagger, his dad is Mick Jagger, and that it's okay, he knows the bank manager.

Patty explains that he will need to secure the loan with some collateral. The frog says, "Sure. I have
this," and produces a tiny porcelain elephant, about an inch tall, bright pink and perfectly formed.

Very confused, Patty explains that she'll have to consult with the bank manager and disappears into a back office.

She finds the manager and says, "There's a frog called Kermit Jagger out there who claims to know you and wants to borrow £30,000, and he wants to use this as collateral."

She holds up the tiny pink elephant. "I mean, what in the world is this?"

The bank manager looks back at her and says."It's a knickknack, Patty Whack. Give the frog a loan, His old man's a Rolling Stone."

A young man goes into a pharmacy and asks the pharmacist:
"Hello, could you give me a condom. My girlfriend has invited me for a Christmas dinner and I think she is expecting something from me!"
The pharmacist gives him the condom; and as the young man is going out, he returns and tells him:
"Give me another condom because my girlfriend's sister is very cute too. She always crosses her legs in a provocative manner when she sees me and I think she expects something from me too."
The pharmacist gives him a second condom; and as the boy is leaving he turns back and says
"After all, give me one more condom because my girlfriend's mom is still pretty cute, and when she sees me she always makes allusions...and since she invited me for dinner, I think she is expecting something from me!!"
During dinner, the young man is sitting with his girlfriend on his left, the sister on his right and the mom facing him. When the dad gets there, the boy lowers his head and starts praying:
"Dear Lord, bless this dinner... thank you for all you give us...!!!"
A minute later the boy is still praying:
"Thank you Lord for your kindness... and ..."
Ten minutes go on and the boy is still praying, keeping his head down. The others
look at each other surprised and his girlfriend even more than the others. She gets close to the boy and whispers in his ear:
"I didn't know you were so religious!!!"

The boy replies:
"I didn't know your dad was a pharmacist"

Jock claims his bagpipes can tell the time. He says he has only to play for a short time and someone will shout 'what idiot's playing the bagpipes at 2:30 in the morning'.

Out with the inlaws last night, I told the Mother in law about our new bedroom drapes, I told her they are thick & heavy & that they were very expensive as they are a direct copy of the one's Henry the Eighth had. & nobody can see what we get up to in the bedroom.
Mother in law said "so you've Tudor curtains?"
I replied "I've even been known to bite her clit"

A couple was celebrating their 30th wedding anniversary. For the entire time they had been married, the wife had kept a safe which the husband had never been allowed to look into. He asked her if, since they had been married so long, he could see what she had been keeping all these years. She said OK and opened the safe. In it were a pile of money totalling £5,000 and three chicken eggs. He asked her, "What are the eggs doing in there?" She said, "Well, I have to admit that I haven't been completely faithful to you. Whenever I strayed, I put an egg in the safe." He thought about it and said, "Well, I guess I can't be too upset about three eggs. But where did all the money come from?" She replied, "Every time I got a dozen, I sold them."

This 80 year old woman was arrested for shoplifting in a supermarket. When she went before the judge he asked her, 'What did you steal?' She replied, 'A can of peaches.'
The judge then asked her why she had stolen the can of peaches, and she replied that she was hungry. The judge asked her how many peaches were in the can. She replied that there were six.
The judge said, 'Then I will give you six days in jail.' Before the judge could actually pronounce the punishment, the woman's husband stood up, and asked the judge if he could say something.
The judge said, 'What is it?' The husband said, 'She also stole a can of peas.'

A man is in bed with his wife when there is a rat-a-tat-tat on the door. He rolls over and looks at his clock, and its half past three in the morning. "I'm not getting out of bed at this time," he thinks, and rolls over. Then, a louder knock follows. "Aren't you going to answer that?" says his wife. So he drags himself out of bed and goes downstairs. He opens the door and there is a man standing at the door. It didn't take the homeowner long to realize the man was drunk. "Hi there," slurs the stranger. "Can you give me a push??" "No, get lost. It's half past three. I was in bed," says the man and slams the door. He goes back up to bed and tells his wife what happened and she says, "Dave, that wasn't very nice of you. Remember that night we broke down in the pouring rain on the way to pick the kids up from the baby sitter and you had to knock on that man's house to get us started again? What would have happened if he'd told us to get lost??" "But the guy was drunk," says the husband. "It doesn't matter," says the wife. "He needs our help and it would be the right thing to help him." So the husband gets out of bed again, gets dressed and goes downstairs. He opens the door, and not being able to see the stranger anywhere he shouts, "Hey, do you still want a push??" And he hears a voice cry out, "Yeah, please." So, still being unable to see the stranger he shouts, "Where are you?" And the stranger replies, "I'm over here, on your swing."

A cabbie picks up a Nun......She gets into the cab, and notices that the VERY handsome cab driver won't stop staring at her. She asks him why he is staring. He replies: 'I have a question to ask you but I don't want to offend you.' She answers, 'My son, you cannot offend me. When you're as old as I am and have been a nun as long as I have, you get a chance to see and hear just about everything. I'm sure that there's nothing you could say or ask that I would find offensive.' 'Well, I've always had a fantasy to have a nun kiss me.' She responds, 'well, let's see what we can do about that: #1, you have to be single and #2, you must be Catholic.' The cab driver is very excited and says,

'Yes, I'm single and Catholic!' 'OK' the nun says. 'Pull into the next alley.' The nun fulfils his fantasy, with a kiss that would make a hooker blush. But when they get back on the road, the cab driver starts crying. 'My dear child,' says the nun, 'why are you crying?'

'Forgive me but I've sinned. I lied and I must confess, I'm married and I'm Jewish.'

The nun says, 'That's OK. My name is Kevin and I'm going to a Halloween party

A Mom visits her son for dinner who lives with a girl roommate. During the course of the meal, his mother couldn't help but notice how pretty his roommate was. She had long been suspicious of a relationship between the two, and this had only made her more curious.... Over the course of the evening, while watching the two interact, she started to wonder if there was more between him and his roommate than met the eye. Reading his mom's thoughts, his son volunteered, "I know what you must be thinking, but I assure you, we are just roommates." About a week later, his roommate came to him saying, "Ever since your mother came to dinner, I've been unable to find the silver plate. You don't suppose she took it, do you?" He said,"Well, I doubt it, but I'll email her, just to be sure." He sat down and wrote : Dear Mother: I'm not saying that you 'did' take the silver plate from my house, I'm not saying that you 'did not' take the silver plate But the fact remains that it has been missing ever since you were here for dinner. Love, your son. Several days later, he received an email from his Mother which read: Dear Son: I'm not saying that you 'do' sleep with your roommate, and I'm not saying that you 'do not' sleep with her. But the fact remains that if she was sleeping in her OWN bed, she would have found the silver plate by now, under her pillow... Love, Mom.

A husband and wife were sitting watching an in depth TV program about psychology that was explaining the phenomenon of mixed emotions. The husband turned to his wife and said, 'Honey, that's a bunch of crap. I bet you can't tell me anything that will make me happy and sad at the same time'.

She said 'Out of all your friends, you have the biggest penis.'

I never have to use Wikipedia because the wife knows it all

A Married Man Was Having an Affair with His Secretary...

...One day they went to her place and made love all afternoon. Exhausted, they fell asleep and woke by 8 in the evening. The man then hurriedly got dressed and asked his lover to take his shoes outside and get those rubbed in the grass and dirt. He then put on his shoes and drove home. Upon reaching there, 'Where have you been?' his wife demanded to know. 'I can't lie to you', he replied,' I'm having an affair with my secretary. We made love all noon.' She then looked down at his shoes and said 'You're a lying bastard! I know you've been playing golf.'

Out walking the dog this morning I went past a giant skip, it was full of Sky remote controls, apparently it was The Man U fans binning their season tickets.

Dear Santa,
How are you? How is Mrs. Claus? I hope everyone, from the reindeer to the elves, is fine. I have been a very good boy this year. I would like an X-Box 360 with Call of Duty IV and an iPhone 4 for Christmas. I hope you remember that come Christmas Day.

Merry Christmas,
Tommy Jones

Dear Tommy,
Thank you for your letter. Mrs. Claus, the reindeer and the elves are all fine and thank you for asking about them. Santa is a little worried about all the time you spend playing video games and texting. Santa wouldn't want you to get fat. Since you have indeed been a good boy, I think I'll bring you something you can go outside and play with.

Merry Christmas,
Santa Claus

Mr. Claus,
Seeing that I have fulfilled the "naughty vs. Nice" contract, set by you I might add, I feel confident that you can see your way clear to granting me what I have asked for. I certainly wouldn't want to turn this joyous season into one of litigation. Also, don't you think that a jibe at my weight coming from an overweight man who goes out once a year is a bit trite?

Respectfully,
Tom Jones

Mr. Jones,

While I have acknowledged you have met the “nice” criteria, need I remind you that your Christmas list is a request and not a guarantee of services provided. Should you wish to pursue legal action, well that is your right. Please know, however, that my solicitors have been on retainer ever since the Burgermeister Meisterburger incident and will be more than happy to take you on in open court. Additionally, the exercise I alluded to will not only improve your health, but also improve your social skills and potentially help clear up a complexion that looks like the bottom of the Burger King frying pan.

Very Truly Yours,
S Claus

Now look here you fat twat. I told you what I want and I expect you to bring it. I was attempting to be polite about this but you brought my looks and my friends
into this. Now you just be disrespecting me. I’m about to tweet my home boys and we’re gonna be waiting for your fat arse and me going to be taking my game console, my game, my phone, and whatever else I want. WHAT EVER I WANT, MAN!

T-Bone Da Terror.

Listen Pizza Face,
Seriously??? You think a Geezer that breaks into every house in the world on one night and never gets caught gives a flying fuck at the moon you yardie tosser wanabee? “He sees you when you’re sleeping; He knows when you’re awake”. Sound familiar, genius? You know what kind of resources I have at my disposal. I got your sh!t wired, you little wanker.I go all around the world and see ways to hurt people that if I described them right now, you’d throw up your K.F.C Bargain Shitbucket all over the carpet of your mother's crappy crack house flat. You’re not getting what you asked for, but I’m still stopping by your gaff to kick a poke hole in your arse and let Rudolf have his jollies. Chew on that Winston!

S Clizzy

Dear Santa,
Bring me whatever you see fit. I’ll appreciate anything.

Tommy

Tommy,
That's what I thought you little bastard.

Santa

Clever Way with Words!

1. ARBITRATOR: A cook that leaves Arby's to work at McDonalds
2. AVOIDABLE: What a bullfighter tries to do
3. BERNADETTE: The act of torching a mortgage
4. BURGLARIZE: What a crook sees with
5. CONTROL: A short, ugly inmate
6. COUNTERFEITERS: Workers who put together kitchen cabinets
7. ECLIPSE: What an English barber does for a living
8. EYEDROPPER: A clumsy ophthalmologist
9. HEROES: What a guy in a boat does
10. LEFTBANK: What the robber did when his bag was full of money
11. MISTY: How golfers create divots
12. PARADOX: Two physicians!!
13. PARASITES: What you see from the top of the Eiffel Tower
14. PHARMACIST: A helper on the farm
15. POLARIZE: What penguins see with
16. PRIMATE: Removing your spouse from in front of the TV!!
17. RELIEF: What trees do in the spring
18. RUBBERNECK: What you do to relax your wife
19. SELFISH: What the owner of a seafood store does
20. SUDAFED: Brought litigation against a government official

Paddy found a pen, he said to Mick 'is it yours'. Mick wrote something on a piece of paper and said 'yes, it's mine'. 'How do you know' said Paddy, Mick said 'it's my handwriting'.

I was in bed with a blind girl last night and she said that I had the biggest penis she had ever laid her hands on. I said, "You're pulling my leg."

I saw a poor old lady fall over today on the ice! At least I presume she was poor - she only had 20p in her purse.

My girlfriend thinks that I'm a stalker. Well, she's not exactly my girlfriend yet.

Went for my routine checkup today and everything seemed to be going fine until he stuck his index finger up my butt! Do you think I should change dentists?

I was explaining to my wife last night that when you die you get reincarnated but must come back as a different creature. She said she'd like to come back as a cow. I said, "You're obviously not listening."

The wife has been missing a week now. Police said to prepare for the worst. So, I've been to the thrift shop to buy all of her clothes back.

At the Senior Citizens Centre they had a contest the other day. I lost by one point: The question was: Where do women mostly have curly hair? Apparently the correct answer was Africa! Who knew?

One of the other questions that I missed was to name one thing commonly found in cells. It appears that Mexicans is not the correct answer either.

There's a new Muslim clothing shop opened in our shopping centre, but I've been banned from it after asking to look at some of the new bomber jackets.

A buddy of mine has just told me he's getting it on with his girlfriend and her twin. I said "How can you tell them apart?" He said "Her brother's got a moustache."

Just put a deposit down on a brand new Porsche and mentioned it on

Facebook. I said, "I can't wait for the new 911 to arrive!" Next thing I know 40,000 Muslims have added me as a friend!

Being a modest man, when I checked into my hotel on a recent trip, I said to the lady at the registration desk, "I hope the porn channel in my room is disabled." To which she replied, "No, it's regular porn, you sick bastard."

The Red Cross have just knocked at our door and asked if we could help towards the floods in Pakistan. I said we'd love to, but our garden hose only reaches the driveway.

I've just paid for my wife and her mother to go to Paris for two weeks. That's how much I hate fucking French.

A woman goes to see a fortune teller. The fortune teller says "I have terrible news. Your husband will die soon, horribly, and in terrible pain." The woman asks "Will I get a Not Proven?"

A football fan is walking home from the match with his supporters gear on. He fancies a drink, walks into a bar only to find himself surrounded by Rival fans.
A deadly silence falls over the pub then the barman clears his throat and says:-
"In here we give you guys a roll of the dice. If you roll 1 to 5, we kill you"
The fan replies, "What happens if I roll a 6?"" The barman replies "You get to roll again."

Q. What do you get if you cross the English cricket team with an OXO cube?
A. A laughing stock.
Q What's the height of optimism?
A: English batsman putting on sunscreen.
Q. What's the difference between an English batsman and a Formula 1 car?
A. Nothing! If you blink you'll miss them both.
Q. What do English batsmen and drug addicts have in common?

A. Both spend most of their time wondering where their next score will come from.
Q. What does an English batsman who is playing in The Ashes have in common with Michael Jackson?
A. They both wore gloves for no apparent reason.
Q. What is the difference between Cinderella and the Pommies?
A. Cinderella knew when to leave the ball.
Q. What's the difference between the Pommies and a funeral director?
A. A funeral director isn't going to lose the ashes.

A DEA officer stopped at a ranch in Texas, and talked with an old rancher. He told the rancher, "I need to inspect your ranch for illegally grown drugs." The rancher said, "Okay, but don't go in that field over there.....", as he pointed out the location. The DEA officer verbally exploded saying, "Mister, I have the authority of the Federal Government with me!" Reaching into his rear pants pocket, the arrogant officer removed his badge and proudly displayed it to the rancher. "See this fucking badge?! This badge means I am allowed to go wherever I wish.... On any land!! No questions asked or answers given!! Have I made myself clear... do you understand?!!" The rancher nodded politely, apologised, and went about his chores. A short time later, the old rancher heard loud screams, looked up, and saw the DEA officer running for his life, being chased by the rancher's big Santa Gertrudis bull...... With every step the bull was gaining ground on the officer, and it seemed likely that he'd sure enough get gored before he reached safety. The officer was clearly terrified. The rancher threw down his tools, ran to the fence and yelled at the top of his lungs..... "Your badge, show him your fucking BADGE!!"

A woman tells her plastic surgeon that she wanted her vaginal lips reduced in size because they had become too loose and floppy. Out of embarrassment she insisted that the surgery be kept a secret and the surgeon agreed. Awakening from the anaesthesia after the surgery, she found 3 roses carefully placed beside her on the bed. Outraged, she immediately calls in the doctor. "I thought I asked you not to tell anyone about my operation!" The surgeon told her he had carried out her wish for confidentiality, and that the first rose was from him: "I felt sad because you went through this all by yourself." "The second rose is from my nurse. She assisted me in the surgery and understood because she had the same procedure done some time ago." "And what about the third rose?" she asked. "That's from a man upstairs in the burns unit. He wanted to thank you for his new ears."

Some bastard's just pinched a pair of my wife's knickers off the washing line.
She's not bothered about the knickers, but she wants the 12 pegs back.

A woman in a hot air balloon realized she was lost. She reduced altitude and spotted a man below. She descended a bit more and shouted: 'Excuse me, can you help me? I promised a friend I would meet him an hour ago but I don't know where I am..'
The man below replied, 'You're in a hot air balloon hovering approximately 30 feet above the ground. You're between 40 and 41 degrees north latitude and between 59 and 60 degrees west longitude.'
'You must be an Engineer,' said the balloonist.
'I am,' replied the man, 'how did you know?'
'Well,' answered the balloonist, 'everything you have told me is probably technically correct, but I've no idea what to make of your information and the fact is, I'm still lost. Frankly, you've not been much help at all. If anything, you've delayed my trip by your talk.'
The man below responded, 'You must be in Management.'
'I am,' replied the balloonist, 'but how did you know?'
'Well,' said the man, 'you don't know where you are or where you're going. You have risen to where you are, due to a large quantity of hot air. You made a promise, which you've no idea how to keep, and you expect people beneath you to solve your problems. The fact is you are in exactly the same position you were in before we met, but now, somehow, it's my fucking fault.

Three friends married women from different parts of the world..... The first man married a Filipino. He told her that she was to do the dishes and house cleaning. It took a couple of days, but on the third day, he came home to see a clean house and dishes washed and put away.
The second man married a Thai. He gave his wife orders that she was to do all the cleaning, dishes and the cooking. The first day he didn't see any results, but the next day he saw it was better. By the third day, he saw his house was clean, the dishes were done, and there was a huge dinner on the table.

The third man married a girl from Glasgow. He ordered her to keep the house cleaned, dishes washed, lawn mowed, laundry washed, and hot meals on the table for every meal. He said the first day he didn't see anything, the second day he didn't see anything but by the third day, some of the swelling had gone down and he could see a little out of his left eye and his arm was healed enough that he could fix himself a sandwich and load the dishwasher. He still has some difficulty when he pees.

I've just been to the gym.
They've got a new machine in.
Only used it for half an hour, as I started to feel sick.
It's great though. It does everything - KitKats, Mars Bars, Snickers, Crisps, the lot.."

Following the tragic death of the Human Cannonball at the Kent Show, a spokesman said "We'll struggle to get another man of the same calibre."

I was devastated to find out my wife was having an affair, but, by turning to religion, I was soon able to come to terms with the whole thing.
I converted to Islam, and we're stoning her in the morning.

The room was full of pregnant women with their husbands.
The instructor said, "Ladies, remember that exercise is good for you. Walking is especially beneficial. It strengthens the pelvic muscles and will make delivery that much easier.
Just pace yourself, make plenty of stops and try to stay on a soft surface like grass or a path.
"Gentlemen, remember -- you're in this together. It wouldn't hurt you to go walking with her. In fact, that shared experience would be good for you both."
The room suddenly became very quiet as the men absorbed this information.
After a few moments a young man slowly raised his hand.

"Yes?" said the Instructor.
"I was just wondering if it would be all right if she carries a golf bag while we walk."

A young man moved out from home and into a new apartment. He went proudly down to the lobby to put his name on his mailbox.
While there, a stunning young lady came out of the apartment next to the mailboxes, wearing only a robe. The boy smiled at the young woman and she started up a conversation with him. As they talked her robe slipped open and it was obvious that she had nothing else on.
The poor kid broke into a sweat trying to maintain eye contact. After a few minutes, she placed her hand on his arm and said,
"Let's go to my apartment, I hear someone coming".
He followed her into her apartment, she closed the door and leaned against it, allowing her robe to fall off completely.
Now nude, she purred at him, "What would you say is my best feature?"
Flustered and embarrassed, he finally squeaked,
"It's got to be your ears".
Astounded and a little hurt she asked, "My ears, look at these breasts, they are a full 38 inches and 100% natural.
I work out every day and my ass is firm and solid. I have a 28 inch waist.
Look at my skin, not a blemish anywhere.
How can you think that the best part of my body is my ears?"
Clearing his throat, he stammered, "Outside when you said you heard someone coming, well that was me.

An Irish daughter had not been home for over 5 years. Upon her return, her father cursed her heavily.
Where have ye been all this time, child?
Why did ye not write to us, not even a line? Why didn't ye call? Can ye not understand what ye put yer old Mother thru?'
The girl, crying, replied, 'Sniff, sniff... Dad.... I became a prostitute.'
'Ye what!!? Get outta here, ye shameless harlot! Sinner! You're a disgrace to this Catholic family..
'OK, Dad... As ye wish. I just came back to give Mum this luxurious fur coat, title deed to a ten bedroom mansion plus a $5 million savings certificate.

For me little brother, this gold Rolex. And for ye, Daddy, the sparkling new Mercedes Limited Edition convertible that's parked outside, plus a membership to the country club... (takes a breath)... And an invitation for ye all to spend New Year's Eve On board my new yacht in the Riviera.'
'Now what was it ye said ye had become?' says Dad.
Girl, crying again, 'Sniff, sniff... a prostitute, Daddy! Sniff, sniff.'
'Oh! Be Jesus! Ye scared me half to death, girl! I thought ye said a Protestant.
Come here and give yer old Dad a hug!!

Fella rang BIRTHS.DEATHS AND MARRIAGES in the Liverpool echo,
he said "how many words for a quid lad?",
the echo worker said "3 why?",
fella says "ok ive only got a quid, put MARY HAS DIED".
So the echo worker feels really sad for the fellah and he said "ok, just have 3 more words, a pound doesn't matter at a time like this, what shall we say in those 6 words?"

So the fella said "MARY HAS DIED, FIESTA FOR SALE"

This says it all really:-

Pythagoras' Theorem: ....24 words
Lord's Prayer: .... 66 words
Archimedes' Principle: ....67 words
Ten Commandments: ....179 words
Gettysburg Address: ....286 words
US Declaration of Independence : ....1,300 words
US Constitution with all 27 Amendments: ....7,818 words
EU Regulations on the Sale of CABBAGES: ....26,911 words

A Scotsman, an Englishman and an Irishman walk into a pub and each order a Pint of Guinness, somewhat improbably a swarm of flies appear and a fly drops into each man's pint.
The Englishman immediately tells the barman that he cannot drink his beer and orders another.
The Scotsman shrugs his shoulders, says "meh" picks the fly out and drinks his pint.
The Irishman grabs the fly by the legs and while shaking it violently utters the words "spit it out ya beggar"

Two elderly nuns are driving late at night. Suddenly the devil appears on the bonnet of their car, gyrating lewdly, his offensively large appendage slapping loudly against the windscreen.
Sister Lucretia tells Sister Absolvia to go faster and say 10 Hail Marys. They do this, but the devil is still there, and if anything his undercarriage is only getting bigger.
"Say 10 Our Fathers," says Sister Absolvia, "and I'll go faster still", and they do, but nothing happens except the Devil's horns (all three of them) just get larger.
Suddenly, Sister Lucretia grabs the crucifix on the rosary beads around her throat and says to Sister Absolvia: "Show him your cross"
So Sister Absolvia leans out the window, grabs her rosary beads and says "Get off the fucking bonnet, ya cunt!"

Have you heard about the new Arsenal bra? It has loads of support but no cups!!

Jack wakes up with a huge hangover after attending his company's Christmas Party. Jack is not normally a drinker, but the drinks didn't taste like alcohol at all.
He didn't even remember how he got home from the party. As bad as he was feeling, he wondered if he did something wrong. Jack had to force himself to open his eyes, and the first thing
he sees is a couple of aspirins, next to a glass of water, on the side table and, next to them, a single red rose! Jack sits up and sees his clothing in front of him, all clean and pressed.
He looks around the room and sees that it is in perfect order, spotlessly clean. So is the rest of the house. He takes the aspirins, cringes when he sees a huge black eye staring back at him in the bathroom mirror. Then he notices a note hanging on the corner of the mirror written in red with little hearts on it and a kiss mark from his wife in lipstick:
"Honey, breakfast is on the stove, I left early to get groceries to make you your favourite dinner tonight. I love you, darling! Love, Jillian"
He stumbles to the kitchen and sure enough, there is hot breakfast, steaming hot coffee and the morning newspaper. His 16 year old son is also at the table, eating. Jack asks, "Son... What happened last night?"
"Well, you came home after 3 a.m., pissed out of your mind, you fell

over the coffee table and broke it, and then you puked in the hallway and got that black eye when you ran into the door.
All in all, one hell of a performance Dad."
Confused, he asked his son, "So, why is everything in such perfect order and so clean?
I have a rose, and breakfast is on the table waiting for me??"
His son replies, "Oh THAT... Mum dragged you to the bedroom, and when she tried to take your trousers off, you screamed...."Leave me alone, I'm married!!"

Broken Coffee Table £239.99
Hot Breakfast £4.20
Two Aspirins £0.38
Saying the right thing, at the right time. . PRICELESS

A guy appears on Stars in Their Eyes. Matthew Kelly tells the audience, "Simon, you have an incredible story, can you tell it to us please?"
"Yes Matthew, about 4 years ago I was involved in a horrific car accident whilst being a passenger in my Uncle Alan's car. Unfortunately Alan lost his life when the steering wheel embedded itself in his chest, my legs were trapped under the dash board and I had to be cut free by the emergency services. In hospital I was told that I would lose both my legs, but by an incredible turn of fate, Alan's lower torso was unharmed and we had the same blood type and marrow match. Then in ground breaking surgery they attached Alan's lower body onto my top half and after 3 years of rehabilitation, I can now run, swim and play football."
"That's a remarkable and brave story, so who are you going to be for us tonight?"
"Tonight Matthew I am going to be Simon and Half Uncle".

I couldn't help but overhear two guys in their mid-twenties, while sitting at a bar. One of the guys said to his buddy, "Man, you look tired."
His buddy said, "Dude I'm exhausted! My girlfriend and I have sex all the time. I just don't know what to do."
An old guy sitting a couple of stools down had also over-heard the conversation. He looked over at the two young men and with the wisdom of years said, "Marry her. That'll put a stop to that shit!"

Its late fall and the Indians on a remote reservation in North Dakota asked their new chief if the coming winter was going to be cold or mild. Since he was a chief in a modern society, he had never been taught the old secrets. When he looked at the sky, he couldn't tell what the winter was going to be like.
Nevertheless, to be on the safe side, he told his tribe that the winter was indeed going to be cold and that the members of the village should collect firewood to be prepared.
But, being a practical leader, after several days, he got an idea. He went to the phone booth, called the National Weather Service and asked, 'Is the coming winter going to be cold?'
'It looks like this winter is going to be quite cold,' the meteorologist at the weather service responded.
So the chief went back to his people and told them to collect even more firewood in order to be prepared.
A week later, he called the National Weather Service again. 'Does it still look like it is going to be a very cold winter?'
'Yes,' the man at National Weather Service again replied, 'it's going to be a very cold winter.'
The chief again went back to his people and ordered them to collect every scrap of firewood they could find.
Two weeks later, the chief called the National Weather Service again. 'Are you absolutely sure that the winter is going to be very cold?'
'Absolutely,' the man replied. 'It's looking more and more like it is going to be one of the coldest winters we've ever seen.'
'How can you be so sure?' the chief asked.
The weatherman replied, 'The Indians are collecting a shitload of firewood'

A thoughtful Scottish husband was putting his coat and hat on to make his way down to the local pub,
He turned to his wee wife before leaving and said, ' Maggie - put your hat and coat on, lassie.'
She replied, 'Aww, Jack that's nice - are you taking me tae the pub wi' ye? '
'Naw,' Jack replied 'Ah'm switching aff the heating while I'm oot.'

He was in ecstasy with a huge smile on his face as his wife moved forward, then backwards, forward, then backwards again......back and forth...back and forth..... in and out..........
She could feel the sweat on her forehead, between her breasts and trickling down the small of her back.
She was getting near to the end.
Her heart was pounding..... Her face was flushed.....
Then she moaned, softly at first, and then began to groan louder.
Finally, totally exhausted, she let out an almighty scream and shouted....

"Okay, Okay!!! I can't park the car!!! You do it, you smug bastard!!!"

What's the difference between a lentil & a chickpea?
I wouldn't pay £200 to have a lentil on my face.

Edinburgh man in hospital on his death bed, surrounded by his Nurse, his Wife Sarah, his daughter Sybil and his sons Bernie and Tam. He is near the end and he asks them to come close. He says 'Bernie, I want you to take Braid Hill Houses. Sybil, I want you to take the flats over Morningside and Bruntsfield. Tam, I want you to take the offices in Charlotte Square. Sarah, my darling wife please take all the residential buildings in New Town.' He then passes away. The Nurse says to his wife 'he must have worked very hard to be able to leave you all that property'. The wife says 'property my arse, the miserable bugger had a paper round'.

A doctor tells me that when he was young he took an entrance exam for medical school. The exam included several questions that would determine eligibility.
One of the questions was: "Rearrange the letters P N E S I to spell an important part of the human body that is more useful when erect."

Those who spelled "SPINE" became doctors... The rest ended up as Members of Parliament.

Local Police hunting the 'knitting needle nutter', who has stabbed six people in the backside in the last 48 hours, believe the attacker could be following some kind of pattern.

Bought some 'rocket salad' yesterday, but it went off before I could eat it!

A teddy bear is working on a building site. He goes for a tea break and when he returns he notices his pick has been stolen. The bear is angry and reports the theft to the foreman. The foreman grins at the bear and says "Oh, I forgot to tell you, today's the day the teddy bears have their pick nicked."

Murphy says to Paddy "What ya talkin to an envelope for?" Paddy replies "I'm sending a voicemail ya thick sod!"

Just got back from my mate's funeral. He died after being hit on the head with a tennis ball.
It was a lovely service.

19 Irish fellas go to the cinema, the ticket lady asks "Why so many of you?"
Mick replies, "The film said 18 or over."

An Asian fellow has moved in next door. He has traveled the world, swum with sharks, wrestled bears and climbed the highest mountain. It came as no surprise to learn his name was Bindair Dundat.

I rang Leeds Arena to book tickets for an Elvis tribute gig today; I was told to press 1 for the money, 2 for the show.....

Bill and his wife Blanche go to the Yorkshire show every year and every year Bill would say,
" Blanche, I'd like to ride in that there 'elicopter "
Blanche always replied,
" I know Bill, but that 'elicopter ride is twenty quid and twenty quid is twenty quid ! "
One year Bill and Blanche went to the fair, and Bill said, " Blanche, I'm 75 years old.
If I don't ride that there 'elicopter, I might never get another chance "
To this, Blanche replied, " Bill that 'elicopter ride is twenty quid, and twenty quid is twenty quid "
The pilot overheard the couple and said," I'll make you a deal. I'll take the both of you for a ride. If you can stay quiet for the entire ride and don't say a word I won't charge you a penny!
But if you say one word it's twenty quid. "
Bill and Blanche agreed and up they went.
The pilot did all kinds of fancy manoeuvres, but not a word was heard.
He did his daredevil tricks over and over again But still not a word...
When they landed, the pilot turned to Bill and said,
" By golly, I did everything I could to get you to yell out, but you didn't I'm impressed! "
Bill replied, " Well, to tell you t'truth I almost said summat when Blanche fell out,
But tha' knows,
twenty quid is twenty quid"

A guy was hunting when a gust of wind blew, the gun fell over & discharged, shooting him in the genitals.
Several hours later, lying in a hospital bed, he was approached by his doctor.
"Well, sir, I have some good news & some bad news.
The good news is that you are going to be OK.
The damage was local to your groin, there was very little internal

damage, & we were able to remove all of the buckshot."
"What's the bad news?" asked the hunter.
"The bad news is that there was some pretty extensive buckshot damage done to your willy which left quite a few holes in it. I'm going to have to refer you to my sister."
"Well, I guess that isn't too bad," the hunter replied.
"Is your sister a plastic surgeon?"
“Not exactly answered the doctor.
"She's a flute player in the Boston Symphony Orchestra. She's going to teach you where to put your fingers so you don't piss in your eye."

How can us fellas ever understand women?
The wife left me a note on the fridge, it read.....
I'm leaving you, I can't take anymore, it's just not working.......
I opened the fridge, the light came on and it was full of beer......
Just what is she going on about????

A few years back, Ian Botham was out having lunch with his wife in a new trendy seafood restaurant, Kathy ordered the sea urchin and Beefy ordered the sea turtle. After a long wait of over half an hour the waiter came to explain that they were having trouble killing the sea turtle as every time its head popped out of its shell and the chef brought down the cleaver the turtle withdrew his head back into its shell. Botham decides to investigate the events in the kitchen and asks the chef if he can have a go. The chef hands over the cleaver and the turtle. Botham very gently inserts his middle finger into the turtles arse and out pops the head long enough for a clean strike and the chef pops the turtle in the pot. Intrigued the chef asks Botham where he had learned to do what he did to the turtle. Botham reply’s “Australia '86, you try getting a tie on Gladstone Small"

"What's the problem?" The doctor asked.
I replied, "When I urinate, it smells of anything that I've eaten or drunk. For instance, if I eat sugar puffs it smells of sugar puffs, or if I drink a chicken Cup-a-Soup it smells of a chicken Cup-a-Soup. What can I do to make my piss smell like piss doctor?"
"Have you tried drinking Foster's?"

Aren't dogs clumsy? I had to free another one that had got its lead entangled round a post outside the local shop. That's the third this week.

A student comes to a young professor's office. She glances down the hall, closes his door, kneels pleadingly.
"I would do anything to pass this exam."
She leans closer to him, flips back her hair, and gazes meaningfully into his eyes.
"I mean" she whispers, "I would do ANYTHING!!"
He returns her gaze. "Anything??"
"Yes. Anything!" She says.
His voice turns to a whisper. "Would you... Study?"

A man received the following text from his neighbour:
I am so sorry Bob. I've been riddled with guilt and I have to confess. I have been tapping your wife, day and night when you're not around. In fact, more than you. I'm not getting any at home, but that's no excuse. I can no longer live with the guilt and I hope you will accept my sincerest apology with my promise that it won't happen again.
The man, anguished and betrayed, went into his bedroom, grabbed his gun, and without a word, shot his wife and killed her.
A few moments later, a second text came in:
Fucking autocorrect. I meant "wifi", not "wife"

I bought my friend an elephant for his room.
He said, "Thanks". I said, "Don't mention it".

STELLA AWARDS:

It's time again for the annual 'Stella Awards'! For those unfamiliar with these awards, they are named after 81-year-old Stella Liebeck who spilled hot coffee on herself and successfully sued the McDonald's in New Mexico, where she purchased coffee. You remember, she took the lid off the coffee and put it between her knees while she was driving. Who would ever think one could get burned doing that, right? That's right; these are awards for the most outlandish lawsuits and verdicts in the U.S. You know, the kinds of cases that make you scratch your head.
Here are the Stellas:

* SEVENTH PLACE *
Kathleen Robertson of Austin, Texas was awarded $80,000 by a jury of her peers after breaking her ankle tripping over a toddler who was running inside a furniture store. The store owners were understandably surprised by the verdict, considering the running toddler was her own son.
Start scratching!

* SIXTH PLACE *
Carl Truman, 19, of Los Angeles, California won $74,000 plus medical expenses when his neighbor ran over his hand with a Honda Accord. Truman apparently didn't notice there was someone at the wheel of the car when he was trying to steal his neighbor's hubcaps.
Scratch some more...

* FIFTH PLACE *
Terrence Dickson, of Bristol, Pennsylvania, who was leaving a house he had just burglarized by way of the garage. Unfortunately for Dickson, the automatic garage door opener malfunctioned and he could not get the garage door to open. Worse, he couldn't re-enter the house because the door connecting the garage to the house locked when Dickson pulled it shut. Forced to sit for eight, count 'em, EIGHT days and survive on a case of Pepsi and a large bag of dry dog food, he sued the homeowner's insurance company claiming undue mental anguish. Amazingly, the jury said the insurance company must pay Dickson $500,000 for his anguish. We should all have this kind of anguish.
Keep scratching. There are more...

* FOURTH PLACE *
Jerry Williams, of Little Rock, Arkansas, garnered 4th Place in the Stella's when he was awarded $14,500 plus medical expenses after being bitten on the butt by his next door neighbor's beagle - even though the beagle was on a chain in its owner's fenced yard. Williams did not get as much as he asked for because the jury believed the beagle might have been provoked at the time of the butt bite because Williams had climbed over the fence into the yard and repeatedly shot the dog with a pellet gun.
Keep scratching...

* THIRD PLACE *
Amber Carson of Lancaster, Pennsylvania received 3rd place because a jury ordered a Philadelphia restaurant to pay her $113,500 after she slipped on a spilled soft drink and broke her tailbone. The reason the soft drink was on the floor: Ms. Carson had thrown it at her boyfriend 30 seconds earlier during an argument.
Only two more so ease up on the scratching...

SECOND PLACE
Kara Walton, of Claymont, Delaware sued the owner of a night club in a nearby city because she fell from the bathroom window to the floor, knocking out her two front teeth. Even though Ms. Walton was trying to sneak through the ladies room window to avoid paying the $3.50 cover charge, the jury said the night club had to pay her $12,000....oh, yeah, plus dental expenses. Go figure.

* FIRST PLACE *
This year's runaway First Place Stella Award winner was: Mrs. Merv Grazinski, of Oklahoma City, Oklahoma, who purchased a new 32-foot Winnebago motor home. On her first trip home, from an Okla.Uni. Football game, having driven on to the freeway, she set the cruise control at 70 mph and calmly left the driver's seat to go to the back of the Winnebago to make herself a sandwich. Not surprisingly, the motor home left the freeway, crashed and overturned. Also not surprisingly, Mrs. Grazinski sued Winnebago for not putting in the owner's manual that she couldn't actually leave the driver's seat while the cruise control was set. The Oklahoma jury awarded her, are you sitting down?
$1,750,000 PLUS a new motor home. Winnebago actually changed their manuals as a result of this suit, just in case Mrs. Grazinski has any relatives who might also buy a motor home.

While walking down the street one day a "Member of Parliament" is tragically hit by a truck and dies. His soul arrives in heaven and is met by St. Peter at the entrance. 'Welcome to heaven,' says St. Peter.. 'Before you settle in, it seems there is a problem. We seldom see a high official around these parts, you see, so we're not sure what to do with you.'
“No problem, just let me in,' says the man.
'Well, I'd like to, but I have orders from higher up. What we'll do is have you spend one day in hell and one in heaven. Then you can choose where to spend eternity.'
Really, I've made up my mind. I want to be in heaven,' says the MP.
'I'm sorry, but we have our rules.' And with that, St. Peter escorts him to the elevator and he goes down, down, down to hell. The doors open and he finds himself in the middle of a green golf course. In the distance is a clubhouse and standing in front of it are all his friends and other politicians who had worked with him.
Everyone is very happy and in evening dress. They run to greet him, shake his hand, and reminisce about the good times they had while getting rich at the expense of the people.
They play a friendly game of golf and then dine on lobster, caviar and champagne.
Also present is the devil, who really is a very friendly & nice guy who has a good time dancing and telling jokes. They are having such a good time that before he realizes it, it is time to go.
Everyone gives him a hearty farewell and waves while the elevator rises....
The elevator goes up, up, up and the door reopens on heaven where St. Peter is waiting for him.
'Now it's time to visit heaven.'
So, 24 hours pass with the MP joining a group of contented souls moving from cloud to cloud, playing the harp and singing. They have a good time and, before he realizes it, the 24 hours have gone by and St.
Peter returns. 'Well, then, you've spent a day in hell and another in heaven. Now choose your eternity.'
The MP reflects for a minute, then he answers: 'Well, I would never have said it before, I mean heaven has been delightful, but I think I would be better off in hell.'
So St. Peter escorts him to the elevator and he goes down, down, down to hell.
Now the doors of the elevator open and he's in the middle of a barren land covered with waste and garbage. He sees all his friends, dressed in rags, picking up the trash and putting it in black bags as more trash falls

from above.
The devil comes over to him and puts his arm around his shoulder.
'I don't understand,' stammers the MP. 'Yesterday I was here and there was a golf course and clubhouse, and we ate lobster and caviar, drank champagne, and danced and had a great time.. Now there's just a wasteland full of garbage and my friends look miserable.
What happened?'
The devil looks at him, smiles and says, 'Yesterday we were campaigning... ...
Today you voted.'

Bloke from Barnsley with piles asks chemist "Nah then lad, does tha sell arse cream?"
Chemist replies "Aye, Magnum or Cornetto?"

A jumbo jet is just coming into the Toronto Airport on it's final approach. The pilot comes on the intercom, "This is your Captain. We're on our final descent into Toronto. I want to thank you for flying with us today and I hope you enjoy your stay in Toronto".
He forgot to switch off the intercom. Now the whole plane can hear his conversation from the cockpit. The co-pilot says to the pilot, "Well, skipper, watcha gonna do in Toronto?"
"Well," says the skipper, "first I'm gonna check into the hotel and take a big crap ... then I'm gonna take that new stewardess with the huge tits out for dinner..... Then I'm gonna wine and dine her, take her back to my room and put it to her big time all night."
Everyone on the plane hears this and immediately begins looking up and down the aisle trying to get a look at the new stewardess. Meanwhile the new stewardess is at the very back of the plane. She's so embarrassed that she starts to run to try and get to the cockpit to turn the intercom off.
Halfway down the aisle, she trips over an old lady's bag and down she goes.
The old lady leans over and says: "No need to hurry, dear. He's gotta take a shit first."

Alex Salmond walks into a Royal Bank to cash a cheque. As he approaches the cashier he says, "Good morning, Ma'am, could you please cash this cheque for me?"
Cashier: "It would be my pleasure sir. Could you please show me your ID?"
Salmond:" Truthfully, I did not bring my ID with me as I didn't think there was any need to. I am Alex Salmond, the leader of the Scottish National Party and First Minister of Scotland!!!!"
Cashier: "Yes sir, I know who you are, but with all the regulations and monitoring of the banks because of impostors and forgers and requirements of the legislation, etc., I must insist on seeing ID."
Salmond: Just ask anyone here at the bank who I am and they will tell you. Everybody knows who I am."
Cashier: "I am sorry, Mr. Salmond, but these are the bank rules and I must follow them."
Salmond: "C'mon lassie. I am urging you, please, to cash this cheque."
Cashier: "Look Mr. Salmond, here is an example of what we can do.
One day, Tiger Woods came into the bank without ID. To prove he was Tiger Woods he pulled out his putter and made a beautiful shot across the bank into a cup. With that shot we knew him to be Tiger Woods and cashed his cheque.
Another time, Andre Agassi came in without ID. He pulled out his tennis racket and made a fabulous shot whereas the tennis ball landed in my cup. With that shot we cashed his cheque.
So, Mr. Salmond, what can you do to prove that it is you, and only you?
Salmond stands there thinking, and thinking, and finally says, "Honestly, my mind is a total blank...there is nothing that comes to my mind. I can't think of a single thing. I have absolutely no idea what to do and I don't have a clue."
Cashier: "Will that be large or small notes, Mr. Salmond?

"A Leeds man walks into a High Street bank & asks for a loan. He tells the bank officer he is going to Australia on business for two weeks & needs to borrow £5,000. The bank officer tells him that the bank will need some form of security for the loan, so the Yorkshire lad hands over the keys and documents of new Ferrari parked on the street in front of the bank. He produces the Log Book & everything checks out. The loan officer agrees to accept the car as collateral for the loan. The bank manager & its officers all enjoy a good laugh at the rough-looking Yorkshireman for using a £120,000 Ferrari as collateral against a £5,000 loan. The bank manager then instructs an employee of the bank to drive the Ferrari into the bank's underground garage, where he parks it. Two weeks later, the man returns, repays the £5,000 & the interest of£15.41.The bank officer says to the Yorkshireman, "Sir, we are very happy to have had your business, & this transaction has worked out very nicely, but we are a little puzzled...While you were away, we checked you out further & found that you are a multi-millionaire. What puzzles us is, why would you bother to borrow "£5,000"? The Yorkshireman replies: "Where else in Leeds can I park my car for two weeks for only £15.41 & expect it to be there when I return"

A Rabbi, Priest and a Presbyterian Minister are attending a Theology seminar and during lunch they engage in a little conversation. The subject of donation comes around and the Minister proudly states "after the collection at Sunday service I put 90% of the collection into the Church for our lord's coffers and keep only 10% for myself towards my expenses". The Priest looks at him as if he's lost the plot and says "Well I work hard for my flock, after the collection at Sunday mass I give 50% to our Father and I keep 50%." Looking round they see the Rabbi smiling, "children", he says, "after the Sabbath collection I take the bowl and throw it high into the air, what stays up is his, what comes down is mine!"

Reminded me of the joke about Paddy in Ireland. Left the pub to go home. It was pouring down with rain. Paddy had had a few and didn't look while crossing the road and got knocked down. His mates in the pub heard the squeal of brakes and they all ran out. Paddy was lying in the puddles on the road. 'Are you all right Paddy' they said. 'Get me the Rabbi' said Paddy. He must have had a bang on the head his friends thought. 'No, you want the priest' they said. 'Bring me the Rabbi' said

Paddy again. 'No, the priest is what you want' they said. 'No, the Rabbi' said Paddy, 'I'm not bringing the priest out on a night like this'.

I asked my Nan if she liked her new stairlift. She said that it's driving her up the bloody wall.

"Sarcasm will get you nowhere in life," my boss told me.
"Well, it got me to the 'International Sarcasm' finals in Santiago, Chile in 2009," I informed him.
"Really?" he asked.
"No," I replied.

My Psychologist says I bear a grudge & have forgiveness issues, ha, we'll see about that.

A Glasgow man phones a dentist to enquire about the cost for a tooth extraction "£85 pounds for an extraction, sir" the dentist replied.
"£85 quid! Huv ye no'got anythin' cheaper?" "That's the normal charge," said the dentist.
"Whit aboot if ye didnae use any anaesthetic?" "That's unusual, sir, but I could do it and would knock £15 pounds off."
"Whit aboot if ye used one of your dentist trainees and still without any anaesthetic?" "I can't guarantee their professionalism and it'll be painful. But the price could drop by £20 pounds."
"How aboot if ye make it a trainin' session, ave yer student do the extraction with the other students watchin' and learnin'?" "It'll be good for the students", mulled the dentist. "I'll charge you £5 pounds but it will be traumatic."
"Och, now yer talkin' laddie! It's a deal," said the Scotsman. "Can ye confirm an appointment for the wife next Tuesday then?"

TEACHER: Why are you late?
STUDENT: Class started before I got here.

TEACHER: John, why are you doing your maths multiplication on the floor?
JOHN: You told me to do it without using tables.

TEACHER: Glenn, how do you spell 'crocodile?'
GLENN: K-R-O-K-O-D-I-A-L'
TEACHER: No, that's wrong
GLENN: Maybe it is wrong, but you asked me how I spell it.

TEACHER: Donald, what is the chemical formula for water?
DONALD: H I J K L M N O.
TEACHER: What are you talking about?
DONALD: Yesterday you said it's H to O.

TEACHER: Winnie, name one important thing we have today that we didn't have ten years ago.
WINNIE: Me!

TEACHER: Glen, why do you always get so dirty?
GLEN: Well, I'm a lot closer to the ground than you are.

TEACHER: Millie, give me a sentence starting with ' I. '
MILLIE: I is.
TEACHER: No, Millie..... Always say, 'I am.'
MILLIE: All right... 'I am the ninth letter of the alphabet.'

TEACHER: George Washington not only chopped down his father's cherry tree, but also admitted it.
Now, Louie, do you know why his father didn't punish him?
LOUIS: Because George still had the axe in his hand.....

TEACHER: Now, Simon, tell me frankly, do you say prayers before eating?
SIMON: No sir, I don't have to, my Mum is a good cook.

TEACHER: Clyde, your composition on 'My Dog' is exactly the same as your brother's.
Did you copy his?
CLYDE: No, sir. It's the same dog.

TEACHER: Harold, what do you call a person who keeps on talking when people are no longer interested?
HAROLD: A teacher.

A husband went to police station for filing a report for his missing wife:

Husband :-I lost my wife, she went shopping and has not returned.

Inspector:-What is her height?

Husband: - I'm not too sure.

Inspector:-Slim or heavy?

Husband: - Not slim exactly.

Inspector:-Colour of eyes?

Husband:-Never noticed.

Inspector:-Colour of hair?

Husband:-Changes according to season.

Inspector:-What was she wearing?

Husband:-Jeans/suit/ I don't remember exactly.

Inspector:-Was she in a car?

Husband:-yes.

Inspector:-tell me the number, name and colour of the car?

Husband:-Black Audi A8 with super charged 3.0 litre V6 engine generating 333 horse power teamed with an eight-speed tiptronic automatic transmission with manual mode. And it has ABS, ESP, parking sensors, GPS, surround sound system, full LED headlights, which use light emitting diodes for all light functions and has a very thin scratch on the front left door. My new custom fit golf clubs, Powacaddy electric trolley are in the boot ....and then the husband started crying...

Inspector:-Don't worry sir, we'll find your car.

Knock on the door today.

As I opened the door I saw a guy in a suit stood there.

"Can I help you?" I asked.

He started taling about the benefits of clean carpets.

Blooy hate Jehoover's witness.

Girl was asked out on a date by a guy with a reputation of being tight fisted. After the date the girl's mother asked how she had got on. The girl said 'he took me out for tea and biscuits, it was quite exciting because I had never given blood before'.

My brother whose mother-in-law lives with him was off last year on a caravan holiday to France for a fortnight with the missus and his 2 small kids. He asked the neighbours to look after his cat (as it was always in their house anyway) and to pop in and check on the mother-in-law every now and again. When he returned home the youngest one jumped out of the car and ran to the neighbours asking where Tibbles was as she had missed him greatly. "Tibbles is dead" he told her bluntly and off she went in hysterical sobbing to her mother. My brother took the neighbour aside and said that he felt he could have handled it a bit better. The neighbour asked how he would had dealt with it? My brother suggested he would have said something along the lines of " I was playing with the cat and it fell off the wall and hurt its leg. I took it to the vet but it got weaker and weaker and after a couple of days the vet said it would be better to put Tibbles out of her misery so she had to be put down." Just at that my sister-in-law came over and asked him if her mother had been any trouble whilst they were away

"Funny you should say that" he said," "I was playing with her and she fell off the wall.............

Jurgen Klopp has ruled himself out of the England manager's job but states his brother Clippety may be interested.

A blond chick gets a job as a physical education teacher of 16 year olds.
She notices a boy at the end of the field standing alone, while
all the other kids are running around having fun kicking a football.
She takes pity on him and decides to speak to him. 'You ok?' she says.
'Yes' he says.
'You can go and play with the other kids you know' she says.
'It's best I stay here' he says.
'Why's that sweetie?' says the blonde.

The boy looks at her incredulously and says: "Because I'm the goalkeeper!"

Shot my first pheasant yesterday. The people in the frozen food section at Harrods panicked a bit.

A man and a woman were sitting beside each other in the first class seating of an airplane.
The woman sneezed, took out a tissue, gently wiped her nose, and then visibly shuddered for ten to fifteen seconds. The man went back to his reading. A few minutes later, the woman sneezed again, took a tissue, wiped her nose, and then shuddered violently once more. Assuming that the woman might have a cold, the man was still curious about the shuddering. A few more minutes passed when the woman sneezed yet again. As before, she took a tissue, wiped her nose, her body shaking even more than before.

Unable to restrain his curiosity, the man turned to the woman and said, "I couldn't help but notice that you've sneezed three times, wiped your nose and then shuddered violently. Are you OK?"
"I am sorry if I disturbed you, I have a very rare medical condition; whenever I sneeze I have an orgasm." The man, more than a bit embarrassed, was still curious. "I have never heard of that condition before" he said.
"Are you taking anything for it?"
The woman nodded,
"Pepper."

A body builder fella, chats up a young blonde, in a bar and persuades her to go back to his place for the evening.
After a couple of drinks and with some sweet music on and the lights turned down low, he takes off his shirt,
and the blonde says,
"What a great chest you have!"
He tells her,
"That's 100 lbs of dynamite, Baby!"
He then takes off his pants and the blonde says,
"What massive calves you have!"
The body builder tells her,
"That's 100 lbs of dynamite, Baby!"
He then removes his underwear and the blonde goes running out of the apartment screaming.
The body builder puts his clothes back on and chases after her.

He catches up to her and asks why she ran out of the apartment like that?
The blonde replies,
"I was afraid to be around all that dynamite, after I saw how short the fuse was!"

On their way to get married, a young Catholic couple are involved in a fatal
car accident. The couple finds themselves sitting outside the Pearly Gates
waiting for St. Peter to process them into Heaven.
While waiting, they begin to wonder: Could we possibly get married in Heaven?
When St. Peter showed up, they asked him. St. Peter says, "I don't know".
This is the first time anyone has asked. Let me go find out", and he leaves.
The couple sat and waited and waited. Two months passed and the couple is
still waiting. As they waited, they discussed that If they were allowed to get married in Heaven, what was the eternal aspect of it all.
"What if it doesn't work?" they wondered, "Are we stuck together FOREVER?"
After yet another month, St. Peter finally returns, looking somewhat bedraggled.
"Yes," he informs the couple, "you CAN get married in Heaven."
"Great!" said the couple, "But we were just wondering, what if things don't
work out? Could we also get a divorce in Heaven?"
St. Peter, red-faced with anger, slams his clipboard onto the ground.
What's wrong?" asked the frightened couple.
"OH, COME ON!" St. Peter shouts, "It took me three months to find a priest
up here!
Do you have ANY idea how long it will take me to find a LAWYER?"

Seamus & Paddy are walking through the countryside, they meet 2 blokes, one has a big bag of freshly caught salmon, the other has a long

length of rope
Seamus says
"Hi fellas where did you get the fish from"?
bloke replies
"About a mile in that direction, you will find a bridge, ah tied the rope around my waist, my mate lowered me over the bridge and ah grabbed the salmon as they tried to swim upstream, then ah shouted my mate who pulled me back up when the bag was full"
Seamus says
"Thanks fellas" "We'll av to try that Paddy"
The blokes offer them the rope and a spare bag.
They accept then set off in search of the bridge.
After walking for 2 miles they discover a bridge, so Seamus ties the rope around Paddy and lowers him over the side.
After about half an hour Seamus hears Paddy shouting, "quick Seamus, pull me up". Paddy says," Have you filled the bag already". "No" said Seamus, "there's a train comin"....

David Cameron is visiting America and Barak Obama takes him to a top secret scientific laboratory. Obama is keen to show off so he shows Cameron a Time Machine that can accurately predict 100 years in the future. 'Ask it a question' says Obama, so Cameron asks 'what will England be like in 100 years' time?' There is a whirring and a bleeping and lights flashing, then a print-out appears. Cameron looks at it for a few minutes and, getting impatient, Obama says 'come on David, what it says'. 'Don't know' says Cameron, 'it's not in English'.

It was hard getting over my addiction to the Hokey Cokey. But I've turned myself around and that's what it's all about.

They just buried the bloke who made the above song.
They put his left leg in, his left leg out. In out, in out, and shook it all about.

I want to live my next life in reverse!

In my next life I want to live my life backwards. You start out dead and get that out of the way. Then you wake up in an old people's home feeling better every day. You get kicked out for being too healthy, go collect your pension, and then when you start work, you get a gold watch and a party on your first day. You work for 40 years until you're young enough to enjoy your retirement. You party, drink alcohol, and are generally promiscuous, then you are ready for high school. You then go to primary school, you become a kid, and you play. You have no responsibilities, you become a baby until you are born. And then you spend your last 9 months floating in luxurious spa-like conditions with central heating and room service on tap, larger quarters every day and then Voila! You finish off as an orgasm!

A man asked his wife, "What would you most like for your birthday?"
She said, "I'd love to be ten again."
On the morning of her birthday, he got her up bright and early and they went to a theme park. He put her on every ride in the park - the Death Slide, The Screaming Loop, the Wall of Fear. She had a go on every ride there was.
She staggered out of the theme park five hours later, her head reeling and her stomach turning.
Then off to a movie theater, popcorn, cola and sweets.
At last she staggered home with her husband and collapsed into bed.
Her husband leaned over and asked, "Well, dear, what was it like being ten again?"
One eye opened and she groaned, "Actually, honey, I meant dress size.

David Cameron asked the Queen,
"Your Majesty, how do you run such an efficient commonwealth and government?
Are there any tips you can give me?"
"Well," said the Queen,
"The most important thing is to surround yourself with intelligent

people."
David Cameron then asked,
"But how do I know if the people around me are really intelligent?"
The Queen took a sip of champagne.
"Oh, that's easy; you just ask them to answer an intelligent riddle, watch me and listen"
The Queen pushed a button on her intercom.
"Please send Prince Charles in here, would you?"
Prince Charles walked into the room and said,
"Yes, Mum?"
The Queen smiled and said to Charles,
"Answer me this please Charlie.
Your mother and father have a child.
It is not your brother and it is not your sister.
Who is it?"
Without pausing for a moment, Prince Charles answered
"That would be me."
"Yes! Very good." said the Queen.
Ah Ha I get it said David, thank you Mam !
And in a great rush he left.
David Cameron went back to Parliament
He decided to ask Nick Clegg the same question.
"Nick, answer this for me."
"Your mother and your father have a child.
It's not your brother and it's not your sister.
Who is it?"
"I'm not sure," said Nick Clegg.
And then in True Nick Clegg Style he went on to say.
"Let me get back to you on that one."
He went to his advisors and asked everyone, but none could give him an answer.
Frustrated, Nick went to the toilet, and found Nigel Farage in there.
Nick Clegg went up to Nigel Farage and asked,
"Hey Nigel, see if you can answer this question."
"Shoot Nick" replied Nigel.
Your mother and father have a child and it's not your brother or your sister.
Who is it?"
Nigel Farage answered, without stalling said;

"That's easy, it's me!"
Nick Clegg grinned, and said,
"Good answer Nigel, I see it all now!"

Nick Clegg then, went back to find David Cameron and said to him;
"David, I did some research, and I have the answer to that riddle."
" If your mother and father have a child who is not your brother or your sister
The Child is Nigel Farage !"
David Cameron went red in the face, got up, stomped over to Nick Clegg, and angrily yelled into his face,
"No! You bloody idiot! It's Prince Charles!"

There was an English guy drowning his sorrows in a pub in Moffat when he decides to drive home. On the A74 he's quickly stopped and the police have a word with him. He's asked to join them in the police car and asked to blow into the breathalyser bag.
At this point he produces a small card, which says:
"The holder of this card is severely asthmatic. Please do not take his breath."
So they cart him off to the police station to get a blood test. They get the doctor in, whereupon he produces another card:
"The holder of this card is severely anaemic. Please do not take his blood."
"Oh well", says the doc, "we'll just have to rely on the urine test."
So then the Englishman produces another card:
"The holder of this card is an England supporter. Please do not take the piss."

A seven year old boy was at the centre of a courtroom drama yesterday when he challenged a court ruling over who should have custody of him. The boy has a history of being beaten by his parents and the judge initially awarded custody to his aunt, in keeping with the child custody law and regulations requiring that family unity be maintained to the degree possible. The boy surprised the court when he proclaimed that his aunt beat him more than his parents and he adamantly refused to live with her. When the judge suggested that he live with his grandparents, the boy cried out that they also beat him. After considering the remainder of the immediate family and learning that domestic violence was apparently a way of life among them, the judge took the unprecedented step of allowing the boy to propose who should have custody of him. After two recesses to check legal references and confer with child welfare officials, the judge granted temporary custody to the England Football team, whom the boy firmly believes are not capable of beating anyone.

Due to England's soul destroying lack of achievement & their early departure from the World cup a number of friendlies have been organised, the first one is on July 26th & is an away match v Iceland, the next one is the following Saturday against Tesco finishing off on Tuesday against ASDA

Guy dies and finds himself stood at the pearly gates. Behind the gates is a wall full of clocks. The guy asks St. Peter what all the clocks are for. St. Peter says that the hands move every time you tell a lie. He points to a clock with the hands on twelve and says ' that is the clock for Mother Theresa and you will see that the hands have never moved'. He points to another with the hands at only two minutes past twelve and says 'that is the clock for Abraham Lincoln and he only told two lies in the whole of his life'. The guy continues to look around and says 'I see you have a ceiling fan'. St. Peter says 'no, that's Tony Blair's clock.

Went for a walk today & I came upon a rather dull looking lantern, being a bit of a collector I decided it might scrub up ok so I gave it a rub with my handkerchief when to my amazement a cloud of smoke appeared then dissipated to reveal a large guy in Egyptian style clothing.
"I am the Genie of the lamp, thank you for releasing me, I can now grant you one wish."
I thought for a moment then said "I want to live forever"
The Genie looked sad & said "I am so sorry but I cannot grant that wish, you must choose another one"
So I gave it a bit more thought & then said "ok I want to live until the

England football team win the World cup"
The Genie looked at me with a knowing grin & said "you crafty bastard"

A Millionaire took his wife to the world cup and decided to pay to have their Rolls Royce flown to Brazil car so they could take in some of the sights in comfort. They were returning to their hotel after England's defeat to Uruguay and noticed a Police car following them. The next thing they knew there were flashing blue lights and they had been pulled over. The Policeman told the guy to wind his window down and was almost bowled over by the smell of alcohol.
Are you sad that your team is out of the world cup asks the Policeman, very shad replies the guy
Have you been drinking to lessen the sorrow my friend asked the Policeman to which the bloke replied yesh I have occifer
How much alcohol have you had tonight asked the Policeman, gallons my friend replied the guy
And what is your intention now sir asks the Policeman, to go back to the hotel and get completely paralytic replies the guy.
The Policeman opens the car door and tells the guy that he has no choice but to arrest him for drink driving and asks if he has anything to say in his defence. Yesh replies the guy, thish is one of the finest cars ever made and its British. That means the steering wheel is on the right and its the wife who is driving so pish off before the bar shuts there's a good chap.

After their arrival in Brazil the Uruguay manager gets the squad together for a bit of a pep talk. Right guys, we need to do well in this world cup for the fans that have come to see us and the fans back home. I expect 100% effort from every player and any player not living up to expectations will be dropped. If we do not get out of the group stages then we will go home in shame and I will have no choice but to look at bringing some new faces in. On hearing this Suarez rises to his feet and asks manager if he can be the first to have one.

A blind guy goes to watch England play and takes his guide dog along. England get a free kick and the dog lets out an almighty howl and nudges his owner. The blind man explains to guy next to him that it is the dogs way of telling him that England have a free kick and the guy next to him looks amazed. The free kick goes in and is cleared by the oppositions defence for a corner. The dog lets out 2 almighty howls and nudges his owner twice. That's his way of telling me that we have a corner he explains. The game ends 0-0 and at the final whistle the dog licks the blind man's hands twice in a circular motion. That is my dog telling me that the result was 0-0. The guy looks stunned and tells the blind man that he wants to sit next to him again in the future as he can't wait to see what the dog does when England win to which the blind man replies 'neither can I mate I have only had him for 5 bleeding years'

Bloke mentioned to his wife that he thought the spark had gone out of their marriage - so she tasered him.

Martha went to her Doctors for a check up on her 60th birthday. The Doctor carried out several tests and told her he would contact her in a week or so with the results. 10 days later Martha got a call to come in and see the Doctor. "Well Martha," he said as she sat down. "I have some bad news for you"
"Go on Doctor, spit it out, I've had a good life so I'm ready." she replied.
"Well Martha, it's not good" he said, "I'm afraid that you are in the early stages of Alzheimer's"
"Oh my" said Martha I have so many memories that's not good, but it sounds like there's something else Doctor"

"Yes Martha, I'm sorry but you also have Parkinson's, I don't know what to say."
"Oh it's Ok Doctor I'm ok, mind you" said Martha "it could be worse"
"how could it be worse?" he asked.
"Well I could have Alzheimer's that would really be a bummer!!!"

My wife says she's divorcing me, because of my obsession with television dramas..........
......but will she really leave me?

Find out next week!

Have you heard the Islamic weather forecast?
It will be mainly Sunni.
But, occasionally Shiite.

A fifteen year old Amish boy and his father were in a mall. They were amazed by almost everything they saw, but especially by two shiny, silver walls that could move apart and then slide back together again.
The boy asked, 'What is this Father?'
The father (never having seen an elevator) responded, 'Son, I have never seen anything like this in my life, I don't know what it is.'
While the boy and his father were watching with amazement, a fat old lady in a motorized cart moved up to the moving walls and pressed a button. The walls opened, and the lady rolled between them into a small room. The walls closed and the boy and his father watched the small numbers above the walls light up sequentially.
They continued to watch until it reached the last number and then the numbers began to light in the reverse order. The doors opened and a beautiful young blonde stepped out.
The father, not taking his eyes off the young woman, said quietly to his son, "Go get your mother"

Once upon a time, a perfect man and a perfect woman met. After a perfect courtship, they had a perfect wedding. Their life together was, of course, perfect.
One snowy, stormy Christmas Eve, this perfect couple was driving their perfect car along a winding road, when they noticed someone at the side of the road in distress. Being the perfect couple, they stopped to help. There stood Santa Claus with a huge bundle of toys. Not wanting to

disappoint any children on the eve of Christmas, the perfect couple loaded Santa and his toys into their vehicle. Soon they were driving along delivering the toys.

Unfortunately, the driving conditions deteriorated and the perfect couple; and Santa Claus had an accident. Only one of them survived the accident.

Question: Who was the survivor?

Answer:

The perfect woman survived. She's the only one who really existed in the first place. Everyone knows there is no Santa Claus and there is no such thing as a perfect man.

**** Women stop reading here, that is the end of the joke.

**** Men keep scrolling.

So, if there is no perfect man and no Santa Claus, the woman must have been driving. This explains why there was a car accident.

By the way, if you're a woman and you're still reading, this illustrates another point: Women never listen.

Australian kids letter home

Dear Mum & Dad,

I am well. Hope youse are too. Tell me big brothers Doug and Phil that the Army is better than workin' on the station - tell them to get in bloody quick smart before the jobs are all gone! I wuz a bit slow in settling down at first, because ya don't hafta get outta bed until 6am. But I like sleeping in now, cuz all ya gotta do before brekky is make ya bed and shine ya boots and clean ya uniform. No bloody horses to get in, no calves to feed, no troughs to clean - nothin'!! Ya haz gotta shower though, but its not so bad, coz there's lotsa hot water and even a light to see what ya doing!

At brekky ya get cereal, fruit and eggs but there's no kangaroo steaks or goanna stew like wot Mum makes You don't get fed again until noon and by that time all the city boys are buggered because we've been on a 'route march' - geez its only just like walking to the windmill in the bullock paddock!!

This one will kill me brothers Doug and Phil with laughter. I keep getting medals for shootin' - dunno why. The bullseye is as big as a bloody dingo's arse and it don't move and it's not firing back at ya like the Johnsons did when our big scrubber bull got into their prize cows before the Ekka last year! All ya gotta do is make yourself comfortable and hit the target - it's a piece of p...!! You don't even load your own cartridges, they comes in little boxes, and ya don't have to steady yourself against the rollbar of the roo shooting truck when you reload!

Sometimes ya gotta wrestle with the city boys and I gotta be real careful coz they break easy - it's not like fighting with Doug and Phil and Jack and Boori and Steve and Muzza all at once like we do at home after the muster.

Turns out I'm not a bad boxer either and it looks like I'm the best the platoon's got, and I've only been beaten by this one bloke from the Engineers - he's 6 foot 5 and 15 stone and three pick handles across the shoulders and as ya know I'm only 5 foot 7 and eight stone wringin' wet, but I fought him till the other blokes carried me off to the boozer.

I can't complain about the Army - tell the boys to get in quick before word gets around how bloody good it is.

Your loving daughter,

Susan xxx

A man in northern Minnesota woke up one morning to find a bear on his roof. He looked in the Yellow Pages, and sure enough, there was an ad for "Up North, Bear Removers." He called the number listed and the bear remover said he'd be over within an hour.
The bear remover arrived, and got out of his van. He had a ladder, a baseball bat, a 12 gauge shotgun, and a mean looking, heavily scarred old pit bull.
"What are you going to do?" the homeowner asked.
"I'm going to put this ladder up against the roof, then I'm going to go up there, and knock the bear off the roof with this baseball bat. When the bear falls off the roof, the pit bull is trained to grab his testicles, and not let go. The bear will then be subdued enough for me to put him in the

cage in the back of the van."
He then handed the shotgun to the homeowner. "What's the shotgun for?" the homeowner asked.
"If the bear knocks me off the roof, you shoot the dog."

A Belfast police officer is standing on a street corner at 3am when he hears the roar of a powerful car coming towards him on a side road. A second later a flash Porsche comes racing up the side road, it slows down at the STOP sign then rolls on through the junction and takes off up the road. The Cop jumps in his police car and chases after the Porsche. A few miles later he stops the car. "Do you know why I've stopped you?" he asks the driver. "No" says the smarmy Londoner as he winks at dumb blonde sitting beside him. You didn't stop at the stop sing back there, you just slowed down." The Cop took his driving licence and walked around the car. While he was away the Londoner says to the blonde "I'll walk rings around this stupid Cop, listen to this" he says. "Hey plod, I slowed down at the sign what's the problem?" he shouted to the Cop. "You didn't stop" came the reply. "I slowed down what's the difference?" he said with a smirk. "Could you please get out of the car?" asks the Cop. The Londoner gets out of his car smiling inanely at the blonde.

At this point the Cop pulls out his baton and proceeds to beat the crap out of the cocky cockney, "now do you want me to stop or just slow down?" he asks

Liverpool airport has been shut for the past 8 hours due to a "Suspicious car".
Apparently it had a tax disc, insurance and the radio was still in it.

There were two men who played golf together every Sunday. One was several strokes better than the other. The lesser player was a proud bugger, and never took any strokes to even up the score.
One Saturday morning, he shows up with a gorilla at the first tee.
He says to his friend, "I've been trying to beat you for so long that I'm aboot ready to give up. But, I heard about this golfing gorilla, and I was wondering if it would be alright if he plays for me today. In fact if you're game, I'd like to try to get back all the money I've lost to you this year. I

sat doon and counted it up last night and it comes tae aboot a £1000. Ye up for it?"

The other guy thought about it for a minute, and then decided to play the gorilla. "How fuckin' good could a gorilla be at golf?" he thought.

Well, the first hole was a straightaway par 4 of 450 yards.

The guy hits a beautiful tee shot, 275 yards down the middle, leaving himself a 6 iron to the green.

The gorilla waddles up to the tee-off, takes a few powerful practice swings and then horses the ball 450 yards, right at the pin, and it stops about 6 inches away from the hole.

The guy turns to his friend and says "That's fuckin' incredible, I would have never believed it if I hadn't seen it wi' my ain eyes. But, you know what, I've seen enough. I've got nae interest in being totally reamed oot by this gorilla golfing machine. You take it back back to where ye got it frae. I need a drink; better make it a double, and I'll write ye oot a cheque for you gettin' back."

The bloke leaves to take the gorilla back, and when he gets back his mate hands over the cheque for the grand and, well into his third double drowning his sorrows, asks, "By the way, how's that gorilla's putting?"

The other guy replies, "Same as his driving."

"That good, eh?"

"Good? Naw. He hits putts the same way - 450 yards, right down the middle!"

Lady fancied a new car, she wanted a real fast sports car. When her husband asked her what she wanted for her birthday, she said 'I'll give you a clue, I want something that goes from zero to 200 in under 4 seconds'. He bought her a set of bathroom scales.

Letter to help line.

Hi Bob

I really need your advice on a serious problem: I have suspected for some time now that my wife has been cheating on me. The usual signs: if the phone rings and I answer, the caller hangs up; she goes out with the girls a lot. I try to stay awake to look out for her when she comes home but I usually fall asleep.

Anyway last night about midnight I hid in the shed behind the boat. When she came home she got out of someone's car buttoning her blouse, then she took her panties out of her purse and slipped them on. It was at that moment crouched behind the boat that I noticed a hairline crack in the outboard engine mounting bracket.

Is this something I can have welded or do I need to replace the whole bracket?

Thanks,

Tom

The wife texted me to say she was in casualty. I switched the TV on and watched it for 50 minutes but didn't see her. She still hasn't come home and I'm starving.

The four Goldberg brothers, Lowell, Norman, Hiram, and Max, invented and developed the first automobile air-conditioner. On July 17th 1946 the temperature in Detroit was 97 degrees.

The four brothers walked into old man Henry Ford's office and sweet-talked his secretary into telling him that four gentlemen were there, with the most exciting innovation in the auto industry, since the electric starter.

Henry was curious and invited them into his office.

They refused and instead asked that he come out to the parking lot to their car.

They persuaded him to get into the car, which was about 130 degrees, turned on the air conditioner, and cooled the car off immediately.

The old man got very excited and invited them back to the office, where he offered them $3 million for the patent.

The brothers refused, saying they would settle for $2 million, but they wanted the recognition by having a label, 'The Goldberg Air-Conditioner,' on the dashboard of each car in which it was installed.

Now old man Ford was more than just a little anti-Jewish, and there was no way he was going to put the Goldberg's name on two million Fords.

They haggled back and forth for about two hours and finally agreed on $4 million and that just their first names would be shown.

And so to this day, all Ford air conditioners show --

Lo, Norm, Hi, and Max -- on the controls.

Fred was in the fertilized egg business. He had several hundred young pullets, and ten roosters to fertilize the eggs. He kept records, and any rooster not performing went into the soup pot and was replaced. This took a lot of time, so he bought some tiny bells and attached them to his roosters. Each bell had a different tone, so he could tell, from a distance, which rooster was performing. Now, he could sit on the porch and fill out an efficiency report, by just listening to the bells. Fred's favourite rooster, old Butch, was a very fine specimen, but this particular morning he noticed old Butch's bell hadn't rung at all! When he went to investigate, he saw the other roosters were busy chasing pullets, bells-a-ringing, but the pullets, hearing the roosters coming, would run for cover. To Fred's amazement, old Butch had his bell in his beak, so it couldn't ring. He'd sneak up on a pullet, do his job and walk on to the next one. Fred was so proud of old Butch, he entered him in the Brisbane City Show and he became an overnight sensation among the judges. The result was the judges not only awarded old Butch the "No Bell Piece Prize," but they also awarded him the "Pulletsurprise" as well. Clearly old Butch was a politician in the making! Who else, but a politician, could figure out how to win two of the most coveted awards on our planet, by being the best at sneaking up on the unsuspecting populace and screwing them when they weren't paying attention.

Vote carefully in the next election, you can't always hear the bells.

The English are feeling the pinch in relation to recent events in Syria and have therefore raised their security level from "Miffed" to "Peeved." Soon, though, security levels may be raised yet again to "Irritated" or even "A Bit Cross." The English have not been "A Bit Cross" since the blitz in 1940 when tea supplies nearly ran out. Terrorists have been re-categorized from "Tiresome" to "A Bloody Nuisance." The last time the

British issued a "Bloody Nuisance" warning level was in 1588, when threatened by the Spanish Armada.

The Scots have raised their threat level from "Pissed Off" to "Let's get the Bastards." They don't have any other levels. This is the reason they have been used on the front line of the British army for the last 300 years.

The French government announced yesterday that it has raised its terror alert level from "Run" to "Hide." The only two higher levels in France are "Collaborate" and "Surrender." The rise was precipitated by a recent fire that destroyed France's white flag factory, effectively paralyzing the country's military capability.

Italy has increased the alert level from "Shout Loudly and Excitedly" to "Elaborate Military Posturing." Two more levels remain: "Ineffective Combat Operations" and "Change Sides."

The Germans have increased their alert state from "Disdainful Arrogance" to "Dress in Uniform and Sing Marching Songs." They also have two higher levels: "Invade a Neighbour" and "Lose."

Belgians, on the other hand, are all on holiday as usual; the only threat they are worried about is NATO pulling out of Brussels.

The Spanish are all excited to see their new submarines ready to deploy. These beautifully designed subs have glass bottoms so the new Spanish navy can get a really good look at the old Spanish navy.

Australia, meanwhile, has raised its security level from "No worries" to "She'll be right, Mate." Two more escalation levels remain: "Crikey! I think we'll need to cancel the barbie this weekend!" and "The barbie is cancelled." So far no situation has ever warranted use of the last final escalation level.

Regards,

John Cleese,

British writer, actor and tall person

My initials are JPH. My middle name is 'Procrastination'. At least it would be if I could be bothered to contact Deed Poll.

You can now get insurance for sex in the UK
Make sure you get the CORRECT insurance for the sex you are having.
Please find a list of companies below catering for most tastes:-
Sex with your wife - Legal & General
Sex with your partner - Standard Life
Sex with someone different - Go Compare
Sex with multiple partners - More Than
Sex on the back seat of a car - Sheila's Wheels
Sex with a prostitute - Commercial Union
Sex with an OAP - Saga
Sex with a transvestite - Confused.com
Sex on the telephone - Direct Line
Sex resulting in pregnancy - General Accident
You should also note that if you are considering
Sex with your maid - Employer's Liability

MAKE SURE YOU ARE ADEQUATELY COVERED

Her - Do you know, I am so ugly?
Me - How do you mean?
Her - My hair is a mess, my eyes are all bloodshot, I have got fat cheeks, three double chins, my boobs are round my waist and I have got a fat bum. Please pay me a compliment Kev.
Me - You've got excellent eyesight.

I was in Hull the other day looking for a B & Q store
after driving around for ages I stopped at the side of the road and asked a local....
"Is there a B & Q in Hull?"
He said "No, Two L's a U and a H"

I tried to order the new ebola band aid song off itunes......
but my anti-virus wouldn't allow it.

A gambler in Northern Ireland was at the horse races playing the ponies and all but losing his shirt.
He noticed a Priest step out onto the track and blessed the forehead of one of the horses lining up for the 4th race.
Lo and behold, that horse - a very long shot - won the race.
Next race, as the horses lined up, the Priest stepped onto the track. Sure enough, he blessed one of the horses.
The gambler made a beeline for a betting window and placed a small bet on the horse.
Again, even though it was another long shot, the horse won the race.
He collected his winnings, and anxiously waited to see which horse the Priest would bless next.
He bet big on it, and it won.
As the races continued the Priest kept blessing long shots, and each one ended up winning.
The gambler was elated.
He made a quick dash to the ATM, withdrew all his savings and awaited for the Priest's blessing that would tell him which horse to bet on...
True to his pattern, the Priest stepped onto the track for the last race and blessed the forehead of an old nag that was the longest shot of the day.
This time the priest blessed the eyes, ears, and hooves of the old nag.
The gambler knew he had a winner and bet every cent he owned on the old nag.
He watched dumbfounded as the old nag came in last.
In a state of shock, he went to the track area where the Priest was.
Confronting Him, he demanded, 'Father! What happened?
All day long you blessed horses and they all won.
Then in the last race, the horse you blessed lost by a mile.
Now, thanks to you I've lost every cent of my savings!'.
The Priest nodded wisely and with sympathy.
'My Son,' he said, 'that's the problem with you Protestants.
You can't tell the difference between a simple blessing and last rites

I've been charged with murder for killing a man with sandpaper.
I only intended to rough him up a bit.

Lawyers should never ask a Georgia grandma a question if they aren't prepared for the answer.

In a trial, a Southern small-town prosecuting attorney called his ...first witness, a grandmotherly, elderly woman to the stand. He approached her and asked, 'Mrs. Jones, do you know me?' She responded, 'Why, yes, I do know you, Mr. Williams. I've known you since you were a boy, and frankly, you've been a big disappointment to me. You lie, you cheat on your wife, and you manipulate people and talk about them behind their backs. You think you're a big shot when you haven't the brains to realize you'll never amount to anything more than a two-bit paper pusher. Yes, I know you.'
The lawyer was stunned. Not knowing what else to do, he pointed across the room and asked, 'Mrs. Jones, do you know the defense attorney?'
She again replied, 'Why yes, I do. I've known Mr. Johnston since he was a youngster, too. He's lazy, bigoted, and he has a drinking problem. He can't build a normal relationship with anyone, and his law practice is one of the worst in the entire state. Not to mention he cheated on his wife with three different women. One of them was your wife. Yes, I know him.'
The defense attorney nearly died.
The judge asked both counselors to approach the bench and, in a very quiet voice, said,
'If either of you idiots asks her if she knows me, I'll send you both to the electric chair.

Went for my eye test appointment today. The nice young girl behind the counter asked me how I was and what could she do for me. I said that I was here for my 1:30 pm eye test. She looked at me carefully and said "Your eyes are really bad sir"
"you can tell that by just looking at me" I replied.
"No," she said, "you're in the newsagents!"

Bill and Jack collared the office junior one lunchtime and instructed him, 'Tek this shilling lad and fetch us three pies - two for us and have one thissen' Twenty minutes later, the lad was back and handed over eight pence to the two men. 'Ey up, what's this then?' asked Jack. 'It's the change' the lad explained, 'they only 'ad one pie left'.

A gang recently broke into a Viagra warehouse.
Police have warned locals to look out for hardened criminals.

That Vincent Van Gogh was in our local the other day.
I asked him if I could buy him a pint and he said "No thanks, I've got one 'ere".

In a Chicago hospital, a gentleman had made several attempts to get into the men's restroom, but it had always been occupied.
A nurse noticed his predicament.
Sir, she said ' You may use the ladies room if you promise not to touch any of the buttons on the wall.'
He did what he needed to, and as he sat there he noticed the buttons he had promised not to touch.
Each button was identified by letters WW, WA , PP, and a red one labelled ATR..
Who would know if he touched them? He couldn't resist.. He pushed WW.
Warm water was sprayed gently upon his bottom.
What a nice feeling, he thought. Men's restrooms don't have nice things like this.
Anticipating greater pleasure, he pushed the WA button. Warm air replaced the warm water, gently drying his underside.
When this stopped, he pushed the PP button. A large powder puff caressed his bottom adding a fragile scent of spring flower to this unbelievable pleasure..
The ladies restroom was more than a restroom, it is tender loving

pleasure.
When the powder puff completed its pleasure, he couldn't wait to push the ATR button which he knew would be supreme ecstasy.
Next thing he knew he opened his eyes, he was in a hospital bed, and a nurse was staring down at him.
'What happened?' he exclaimed. The last thing I remember was pushing the ATR button.

'The button ATR is an Automatic Tampon Remover. Your penis is under your pillow.'

Dave was bragging to his boss one day, "You know, I know everyone there is to know. Just name someone, anyone, and I know them."
Tired of his boasting, his boss called his bluff, "OK, Dave, how about Tom Cruise?"
"No dramas boss, Tom and I are old friends, and I can prove it."
So Dave and his boss fly out to Hollywood and knock on Tom Cruise's door, and Tom Cruise shouts, "Dave! What's happening? Great to see you! Come on in for a beer!"
Although impressed, Dave's boss is still sceptical. After they leave Cruise's house, he tells Dave that he thinks him knowing Cruise was just lucky.
"No, no, just name anyone else," Dave says.
"President Obama," his boss quickly retorts. "Yup," Dave says, "Old buddies, let's fly out to Washington," and off they go. At the White House, Obama spots Dave on the tour and motions him and his boss over, saying, "Dave, what a surprise, I was just on my way to a meeting, but you and your friend come on in and let's have a cup of coffee first and catch up."
Well, the boss is very shaken by now but still not totally convinced. After they leave the White House grounds he expresses his doubts to Dave, who again implores him to name anyone else.
"The Pope," his boss replies.
"Sure!" says Dave. "I've known the Pope for years." So off they fly to Rome.
Dave and his boss are assembled with the masses at the Vatican's St. Peter's Square when Dave says, "This will never work. I can't catch the Pope's eye among all these people. Tell you what, I know all the guards so let me just go upstairs and I'll come out on the balcony with the Pope."

He disappears into the crowd headed towards the Vatican.
Sure enough, half an hour later Dave emerges with the Pope on the balcony, but by the time Dave returns, he finds that his boss has had a heart attack and is surrounded by paramedics.
Making his way to his boss' side, Dave asks him, "What happened?"
His boss looks up and says, "It was the final straw... you and the Pope came out on to the balcony and the man next to me said, 'Who the HECK is that on the balcony with Dave?'

I was walking past our local mental hospital the other day, the patients were the other side of the fence shouting, 13, 13, 13, 13.
The fence was too high to look over so I took a peep through a knot whole, some idiot poked me in the eye, everyone then shouted, 14,14,14,14

BIOLOGY EXAM.
This is straight from Scotland.
Students in an advanced Biology class were taking their mid-term exam.
The last question was, 'Name seven advantages of Mother's Milk.
The question was worth 70 points or none at all.
One student, in particular, was hard put to think of seven advantages.
However, he wrote:
1) It is perfect formula for the child.
2) It provides immunity against several diseases.
3) It is always the right temperature.
4) It is inexpensive.
5) It bonds the child to mother, and vice versa.
6) It is always available as needed.
7) It comes in two attractive containers and its high enough off the ground where the cat can't get it.

He got an A.

Had a major development in my life recently. Things will never be the same. I've bought a universal remote - the moment I saw it I thought 'this changes everything'

Had a power cut today. Lap-top didn't work, TV didn't work, couldn't play golf as it was pouring down. Decided to make a coffee but the kettle didn't work. Chatted to the wife for a couple of hours and she seems quite a nice person.

My son's been asking me for a pet spider for his birthday, so I went to our local pet shop and they were £70!! To hell with that, I thought.
I can get one cheaper off the web.

The local news station was interviewing an 80-year-old lady because she had just gotten married for the fourth time. The interviewer asked her questions about her life, about what it felt like to be marrying again at 80, and then about her new husband's occupation.
"He's a funeral director," she answered.
"Interesting," the newsman thought.
He then asked her if she wouldn't mind telling him a little about her first three husbands and what they did for a living. She paused for a few moments, needing time to reflect on all those years. After a short time, a smile came to her face and she answered proudly, explaining that she had first married a banker when she was in her 20's, then a circus ringmaster when in her 40's, and a preacher when in her 60's, and now in her 80's - a funeral director.
The interviewer looked at her, quite astonished, and asked why she had married four men with such diverse careers.
She smiled and explained, "I married one for the money, two for the show, three to get ready, and four to go."

I used to have a job drilling holes for water. It was well boring.

I got stuck in a traffic jam. The traffic report said the road workers had played two games of football, in dance costumes, on the gravel. And the sports report confirmed, it was tu-tu on aggregate.

I'm not very tech savvy. Maybe it's my age. I've been trying to download this video on incontinence. Problem is, it's just continually streaming.

My friend has a daily blog, posting at length about her breakfast. It's always nothing but waffle.

I got into a pointless argument with the manager at the local garden centre, when he suggested I needed decking.

I have a very cute kitten, but he does get everywhere. Recently, he got his feet caught under my Sky Box, and now my telly's permanently on paws.

My Roman friend won't go and see the film Poison Ivy until he's been to see the films Poison 1 ...

If you take a Daily Mirror poll, you may find that most of its readers are Labour party supporters. If you take a Telegraph poll, you may find that most of your wires fall down.

A guy walks into a pub with a biscuit tin and a duck, puts the tin on the bar and the duck on the tin and immediately the duck starts dancing. Barman says "That's good, must be quite a crowd puller". "Yep, people will stand and watch it all day" replied the man. Sure enough the pub quickly filled with people wanting to see the dancing duck, and who then spent lots of money in the bar. Barman says "Do you fancy selling the duck" so a deal is done, and as the man leaves he says "The duck will only dance on that tin so keep them together and if you have any problems, phone me". The bar man then closes the pub, and sits back

and
counts his takings whilst the duck still dances. After an hour, the duck is still
dancing and the bar man thinks "how can I stop the duck from dancing, the guy
told me to keep them together so what do I do". All night the bar man lays in
bed listening to the rattle of webbed feet on an empty tin, till eventually he phone
the guy and says "How the hell do I stop this bloody duck from dancing", Did
you take the lid of the tin?" asks the guy, "Why" said the barman,
"Cos then you can blow the candle out"

We had a mega localised storm. Gale force winds, torrential rain, sleet, and hailstones. The wife spent ages looking through the window. After an hour I thought I better let her in.

One day a florist went to a barber for a haircut. After the cut, he asked about his bill, and the barber replied, 'I cannot accept money from you; I'm doing community service this week.' The florist was pleased and left the shop. When the barber went to open his shop the next morning, there was a 'thank you' card and a dozen roses waiting for him at his door.

Later, a cop comes in for a haircut, and when he tries to pay his bill, the barber again replied, 'I cannot accept money from you; I'm doing community service this week.' The cop was happy and left the shop. The next morning when the barber went to open up, there was a 'thank you' card and a dozen doughnuts waiting for him at his door?

Then an MP came in for a haircut, and when he went to pay his bill, the barber again replied, 'I cannot accept money from you. I'm doing community service this week' The MP was very happy and left the shop. The next morning, when the barber went to open up, there were a dozen MPs lined up waiting for a free haircut.

And that, my friends, illustrates the fundamental difference between the citizens of our country and the politicians who run it.

Tips for life
Nine important facts to remember, as we grow older:
Number 9 - Death is the number 1 killer in the world.
Number 8 - Life is sexually transmitted.
Number 7 - Good health is merely the slowest possible rate at which one can die.
Number 6 - Men have two emotions: hungry and horny, and they can't tell them apart. If you see a gleam in his eyes, make him a sandwich.
Number 5 - Give a person a fish and you feed them for a day. Teach a person to use the Internet and they won't bother you for weeks, months or maybe even years.
Number 4 - Health nuts are going to feel stupid someday, lying in the hospital, dying of nothing.
Number 3 - All of us could take a lesson from the weather. It pays no attention to criticism.
Number 2 - In the 60's, people took acid to make the world weird. Now the world is weird, and people take Prozac to make it normal.
Number 1 - Life is like a jar of jalapeno peppers. What you do today might burn your ass tomorrow.
...and as someone recently said to me: Don't worry about old age; it doesn't last that long

A mother-in-law stopped by unexpectedly the recently married couple's house. She knocks on the door, then immediately walks in. She is shocked to see her daughter-in-law lying on the couch, totally naked.
"What are you doing?" she asked.
"I'm waiting for Jeff to come home from work," the daughter-in-law answered.
"But you're naked!" the mother-in-law exclaimed.
"This is my love dress," the daughter-in-law explained.
"Love dress? But you're naked!"
"Jeff loves me to wear this dress! It makes him happy and it makes me happy."
The mother-in-law on the way home thought about the love dress. When she got home she got undressed, showered, put on her best perfume and expectantly waited for her husband, lying provocatively on the couch.
Finally her husband came home. He walked in and saw her naked on the couch.
"What are you doing?" he asked.

"Needs ironing," he says" "What's for dinner?"

After a tiring day, a commuter settled down in his seat and closed his eyes.
As the train rolled out of the station, a woman sitting next to him pulled out her mobile phone.
She started talking in a loud voice: "Hi sweetheart. It's Sue. I'm on the train". "Yes, I know it's the six thirty and not the four thirty, but I had a long meeting. No, honey, not with that Kevin from the accounting office. It was with the boss. No sweetheart, you're the only one in my life. Yes, I'm sure, cross my heart!"
Fifteen minutes later, she was still talking loudly. When the man sitting next to her had enough, he leaned over and said into the phone, "Sue, hang up the phone and come back to bed."
Sue doesn't use her mobile phone in public any longer.

Bloke goes in to the doctor's and says 'Doctor I can't stop mentioning the names of Scandinavian capital cities when I talk'
"That's worrying' says the quack 'Are you under a lot of pressure at work at the moment?'
'No' says the bloke 'I used to work in a warehouse for Ikea, but I got sacked for taking Stockholm'

Argentina are due to play Scotland, Messi walks into the dressing room and sees all his team-mates looking glum.
"What's the matter lads?"
"To be honest Lionel we're finding it hard to motivate ourselves, it's p**sing down with rain and Scotland are so c**p that we're just not feeling it"
Messi thinks for a second then says "You know what lads, I reckon I can beat Scotland by myself, you all head down to the pub and I'll meet you after."
So all the players head down the pub and Messi heads out to the pitch. 10 minutes into the game and the players check the score and see the score Scotland - 0, Argentina - 1 (Messi, 8 minutes)

The players go mad "I can't believe he's winning!". They quickly start getting drinks in and forget about the match. Later they realise that the match must be finished so check the scores.
Scotland - 1 (McAndrews, 89 minutes), Argentina - 1 (Messi, 8 minutes)
"Unbelievable, he's got a draw all by himself!"
They all head back to the changing rooms to celebrate and see Messi looking sad with his head in his hands.
'Cheers up, you've just got a draw all by yourself! "
"I'm sorry lads I let you all down"
"Don't be silly, how?"
"I got sent off after 12 minutes"

What do you call a snobbish prisoner walking down some stairs?
A condescending con descending.

A large woman, wearing a sleeveless sundress, walked into a bar in Dublin, Ireland.
She raised her right arm, revealing a huge, hairy armpit as she pointed to all the people sitting at the bar and asked, "What man here will buy a woman a drink?"
The bar went silent as the patrons tried to ignore her. But down at the end of the bar, an owl-eyed drunk slammed his hand down on the counter and bellowed, "Give the ballerina a drink!" The bartender poured the drink, and the woman chugged it down. She turned to the patrons and again pointed around at all of them, revealing the same hairy armpit, and asked, "What man here will buy a lady another drink? “Once again, the same little drunk slapped his money down on the bar and said, "Give the ballerina another drink! “The bartender approached the little drunk and said, "Tell me, Paddy, it's your business if you want to buy the lady a drink, but why do you keep calling her the ballerina?" The drunk replied,
"Any woman who can lift her leg that high has got to be a ballerina!"?

I took the shell off my racing snail, to see if it would make him move any faster?
If anything, though, it's just made him more sluggish.

A chap walks into an Indian restaurant & asks for a Chicken Tarka. The waiter says does Sir mean a Chicken Tikka no replies the customer this one's a little otter.

The life of a snail is taken with a pinch of salt.

I saw 2 snails fighting in my garden. I was going to part them, but in the end I let them slug it out.

Sat opposite an Indian lady on the train today, she shut her eyes and stopped breathing.
I thought she was dead, until I saw the red spot on her forehead and realised she was just on standby.

Couple turn up at a party, the man carrying the woman into the house piggy-back style.
The host asks "Why aren't you dressed up? It's fancy dress tonight!"
"We know ..." replies the man. "I've come as a snail. This is Michelle!"

Two policemen call the station on the radio.
"Hello. Is that the Sarge?"
"Yes?"
"We have a case here. A woman has shot her husband for stepping on the floor she had just mopped clean."
"Have you arrested the woman?"
"No sir. The floor is still wet.

People in the UK eat more bananas than monkeys.
In 2014, they ate 126,472,925 bananas but only 6 monkeys.

A guy brings his best mate home, unannounced, for dinner at 6:30. His wife screams her head off while his friend sits open mouthed and listens to the tirade.
"My bloody hair & makeup are not done, the house is a complete mess, and the dishes aren't done. Can't you see I'm still in my pyjamas and I can't be bothered with cooking tonight! Why the hell did you bring him home unannounced, you stupid idiot?"
"Because he's thinking of getting married.

British Army based in the African Jungle in the 1920's. Regimental Colonel is going back to the UK and his replacement arrives. They have their gin and tonics and cucumber sandwiches and the Colonel says 'let me introduce you to my right hand man, the Adjutant, Captain Smithers. In comes Smithers. Three feet tall, hunch back, bald, no teeth, withered arm. 'Tell the new C O about yourself' says the Colonel. 'Well' says Captain Smithers, I was top of the intake at Sandhurst, won the MC at the Somme, and was mentioned in dispatches five times........ 'No' said the Colonel, 'he can read all that in your records, I meant tell him about the time you told the witch doctor to fuck off'.

So I was getting into my car, and this bloke says to me "Can you give me a lift?" I said "Sure, you look great, the world's your oyster, go for it.'"
"You know, somebody actually complimented me on my driving today. They left a little note on the windscreen, it said 'Parking Fine.' So that was nice."
I had a note like that once. They were so nice that they said if I paid it in 2 weeks, I only had to pay half. So that was nice!
I bought some Armageddon cheese today, and it said on the packet 'Best Before End...'
So I went to buy a watch, and the man in the shop said "Analogue." I said "No, just a watch."
So I went in to a pet shop. I said, "Can I buy a goldfish?" The guy said, "Do you want an aquarium?" I said, "I don't care what star sign it is."
So I went down the local supermarket, I said "I want to make a

complaint, this vinegar's got lumps in it", he said "Those are pickled onions".
I was having dinner with my boss and his wife and she said to me, "How many potatoes would you like?". I said "Ooh, I'll just have one please". She said "It's OK, you don't have to be polite" "Alright" I said "I'll just have one then, you stupid cow"
So I went to the dentist. He said "Say Aaah." I said "Why?" He said "my dog's died.'"
"Now, most dentist's chairs go up and down, don't they? The one I was in went back and forwards. I thought 'This is unusual'. And the dentist said to me, get out of the filing cabinet.'"
"So I got home, and the phone was ringing. I picked it up, and said 'Who's speaking please?' And a voice said 'You are.'"
"So I rang up my local swimming baths. I said 'Is that the local swimming baths?' He said 'It depends where you're calling from.'"
So I told my girlfriend I had a job in a bowling alley. She said "Tenpin?" I said, "No, it's a permanent job."
A friend of mine always wanted to be run over by a steam train. When it happened, he was chuffed to bits!
So I went to the record shop and I said "What have you got by The Doors?" He said: "A bucket of sand and a fire blanket!"
I was in the army once and the Sergeant said to me: "What does surrender mean?" I said: "Oh ... I give up!"
I bought some HP sauce the other day. It's costing me 6p a month for the next 2 years.
I went to buy some camouflage trousers the other day but I couldn't find any.
Police arrested two kids yesterday, one was drinking battery acid, the other was eating fireworks. They charged one and let the other one off.
Two fish in a tank, one says to the other - you drive I'll man the guns

"My dog just chased some kid on a bike"
"Wow, I had no idea your dog could even ride a bike..."

I saw this bloke chatting up a cheetah, I thought
"he's trying to pull a fast one".

I took a sweet along to Antiques Roadshow today, to get it valued?
Mr Expert said "Well I can see it's a Werthers, but I'm not sure it's an original?"

I was in Sydney at the Rocks last night, standing at the bar waiting for a beer, when a butt-ugly, big old heifer came up behind me, and slapped me on the arse.
She said, *"Hey sexy, how about giving me your number!"*
I looked at her and said, *"Have you got a pen?"*
She said, *"I sure do."*
I said, *"Well, you better get back into it before the farmer notices you're missing."*

My wife said to me, "I'm fed up with you being so lazy, pack your bags and leave."
I said, "You pack them."

Actual travel complaints

> "On my holiday to Goa in India, I was disgusted to find that almost every restaurant served curry. I don't like spicy food."
> "They should not allow topless sunbathing on the beach. It was very distracting for my husband who just wanted to relax."
> "We went on holiday to Spain and had a problem with the taxi drivers as they were all Spanish."
> "We booked an excursion to a water park but no-one told us we had to bring our own swimsuits and towels. We assumed it would be included in the price."
> "The beach was too sandy. We had to clean everything when we returned to our room."
> "We found the sand was not like the sand in the brochure. Your

brochure shows the sand as white but it was more yellow."
"It's lazy of the local shopkeepers in Puerto Vallarta to close in the afternoons. I often needed to buy things during 'siesta' time -- this should be banned."
"No-one told us there would be fish in the water. The children were scared."
"Although the brochure said that there was a fully equipped kitchen, there was no egg-slicer in the drawers."
"I think it should be explained in the brochure that the local convenience store does not sell proper biscuits like custard creams or ginger nuts."
"The roads were uneven and bumpy, so we could not read the local guide book during the bus ride to the resort. Because of this, we were unaware of many things that would have made our holiday more fun."
"It took us nine hours to fly home from Jamaica to England. It took the Americans only three hours to get home. This seems unfair."
"I compared the size of our one-bedroom suite to our friends' three-bedroom and ours was significantly smaller."
"The brochure stated: 'No hairdressers at the resort.' We're trainee hairdressers and we think they knew and made us wait longer for service."
"When we were in Spain, there were too many Spanish people there. The receptionist spoke Spanish, the food was Spanish. No one told us that there would be so many foreigners."
"We had to line up outside to catch the boat and there was no air-conditioning."
"It is your duty as a tour operator to advise us of noisy or unruly guests before we travel."
"I was bitten by a mosquito. The brochure did not mention mosquitoes."
"My fiancée and I requested twin-beds when we booked, but instead we were placed in a room with a king bed. We now hold you responsible and want to be re-reimbursed for the fact that I became pregnant. This would not have happened if you had put us in the room that we booked."

Far away in the tropical waters of Australia, two prawns were swimming around in the sea -
one called Justin and the other called Christian.
The prawns were constantly being harassed and threatened by

sharks that patrolled the area.
Finally one day Justin said to Christian, "I'm bored and frustrated at being a prawn, I wish I was a shark,
then I wouldn't have any worries about being eaten..."
Just as Justin had his mind firmly on becoming a predator, a mysterious cod appears and says,
"Your wish is granted", and lo and behold, Justin turned into a shark.
Horrified, Christian immediately swam away, afraid of being eaten by his old mate.
Time went on (as it invariably does...) and Justin found himself becoming bored and lonely as a shark.
All his old mates simply swam away whenever he came close to them.
Justin realised that his new menacing appearance was the cause of his sad plight.
While out swimming alone one day he sees the mysterious cod again and can't believe his luck.
Justin figured that the fish could change him back into a prawn.
He begs the cod to change him back so, lo and behold, he is turned back into a prawn.
With tears of joy in his tiny little eyes, Justin swam back to his friends and bought them all a cocktail.
(The punch line does not involve a prawn cocktail - it's much worse).
Looking around the gathering at the reef, he searched for his old pal. "Where's Christian?" he asked.
"He's at home, distraught that his best friend changed sides to the enemy and became a shark", came the reply.
Eager to put things right again and end the mutual pain and torture, he set off to Christian's house.
As he opened the coral gate the memories came flooding back.
He banged on the door and shouted,
"It's me, Justin, your old friend, come out and see me again."
"Christian replied "No way man, you'll eat me. You're a shark, the enemy and I'll not be tricked."
Justin cried back "No, I'm not. That was the old me. I've changed."
"I've found Cod, I'm a prawn again Christian".

There was a man who loved tractors, I mean he absolutely LOVED them. He had tractor models, tractor wallpaper, remote control miniature tractors, tractor board games, every home and away shirt, even some tractor porn (which is not easy to find mind you). The only thing that even came close to his love for tractors was the love he felt for his wife. His high school sweetheart, who didn't mind his infatuation with tractors one bit. She didn't even mind the role play where she would dress as a tractor, he would dress as a farmer, and he would take her for a "ride".
Sadly his wife was struck one day, a tractor fell right off the back of a transport truck. She didn't die until he was at her side in the hospital. Her dying words *"please don't blame the tractor honey"* and with that she headed to the big farm in the sky.
Sadly, he *did* blame the tractor, he hated them now with all his mind, body, and soul. He went home and destroyed ALL his tractor related items, the toys, his wife's tractor suit even his collection of tractor porn. He put it all in a pile and burned it in the yard.
Whatever didn't burn enough to his liking was thrown into a woodchipper. He then went inside, rarely leaving his home, for 8 years. Finally on the 8th anniversary of his darling wife's death he decided it was time to get back out in the dating world, plus the cute cashier at the grocery store had been asking him out for a while now, he called her out to dinner.
The restaurant he choose ended up being quite nice, good food, good service, great decor. But there was one problem, it was EXTREMELY smoky. So smoky that his date, being an asthmatic, was having some trouble breathing. After noticing her displeasure, and trouble breathing, he started breathing in. I mean REALLY breathing in. Inhaling with such force that all the smoke quickly left the dining room, and went into his lungs. When the room was void of smoke he stepped outside and released it all into the night. When he rejoined his date she asked "how on earth did you do that?" to which he replied, ***"I'm an extractor fan."***

Gervais is a restaurateur.
He owns a fantastically successful French bistro on the Med which is packed out every night of the week.
It has an international reputation for excellence and such is the fame of his legendary seafood dishes people come all over the

planet to try them.
In pride of place, at the front of house, there's a giant, gleaming tank, teeming with all kinds of fresh fish and treasures of the sea, many of them caught that very morning. People can pick and choose whatever crab, lobster, cuttlefish or other seafood creature they fancy and though the wait is a little longer than usual, they know they're getting the very freshest catch of the day.
There is, however, one slightly odd-looking, green-coloured squid and, what's more, he sports a resplendent moustache. A proper handlebar affair.
It's a completely unique animal and is a bit of a celebrity around the resort. Nobody has ever chosen it for obvious reasons and he's resided happily in the restaurant for many years, becoming a mascot with the staff and clientele.
One day, the unthinkable happens: a drunken, colour-blind Scotsman asks for the thing to be cooked.
The staff are taken aback.
Nobody wants to tell Gervais - his infamous temper is almost as well renowned as his food - but as, technically, everything in the tank is there to be eaten, it falls upon the chef to remove the funny little cephalopod and take him to the kitchen to be prepared and cooked.
The chef never actually takes anything from the tank himself - he's far too talented and important to lower himself to mere menial tasks - so, as usual, he asks the Austrian washer-upper, Hans, to do it.
Once out the back, Hans gently lays the little fella on a chopping board and looks across at the chef, who gives him a solemn nod authorising Hans to slice up the creature ready for the pan. Five minutes. For a full five minutes, Hans is there, standing over his pale green friend from the sea. He's physically shaking and actually crying when Gervais himself storms into the kitchen - he's just heard the news!
"I am a businessman. You know how this works! You must kill the thing so chef can cook it. Come on! Chop, chop!!"
"But I can't do it ... don't make me do it ..." Hans cries, as he puts down the cleaver and drops to his knees.
"Useless washer-upper! I suppose I'll have to do it myself!!" Gervais bellows as he pushes the Austrian out of the way.
He picks up the knife, squares the creature on the board, raises his arm ... and then also drops to his knees, crying, embracing Hans and the chef, all of them too distraught to hurt the little

guy ...
The moral of the story?
Well, it's this:

Hans that do dishes is as soft as Gervais with the pale-green, furry-lipped squid ...

As a butcher is shooing a dog from his shop, he sees £10 and a note in his mouth, reading: "10 lamb chops, please."
Amazed, he takes the money, puts a bag of chops in the dog's mouth, and quickly closes the shop.
He follows the dog and watches him wait for a green light, look both ways, and trot across the road to a bus-stop.
The dog checks the timetable and sits on the bench.
When a bus arrives, he walks around to the front and looks at the number, then boards the bus.
The butcher follows, dumbstruck. As the bus travels out into the suburbs, the dog takes in the scenery.
After a while he stands on his back paws to push the "stop" bell, and then the butcher follows him off.
The dog runs up to a house and drops his bag on the step. He barks repeatedly.
No answer.
He goes back down the path, takes a big run, and throws himself -Whap!- against the door. He does this again & again.
No answer.
So he jumps on a wall, walks around the garden, barks repeatedly at a window, jumps off, and waits at the front door.
Eventually, a small guy opens it and starts cursing and shouting at the dog.
The butcher runs up screams at the guy: "What the hell are you doing? This dog's a genius!"
The owner responds, "Genius, my arse. It's the second time this week he's forgotten his key.

The old man placed an order for one hamburger, French fries and a drink.
He unwrapped the plain hamburger and carefully cut it in half, placing one
half in front of his wife.

He then carefully counted out the French fries, dividing them into two piles and neatly placed one pile in front of his wife.
He took a sip of the drink, his wife took a sip and then set the cup down between them.
As he began to eat his few bites of hamburger, the people around them were looking over and whispering.
Obviously they were thinking, 'That poor old couple - all they can afford is one meal for the two of them.'
As the man began to eat his fries, a young man came to the table and politely offered to buy another meal for the old couple.
The old man said, they were just fine - they were used to sharing everything.
People closer to the table noticed the little old lady hadn't eaten a bite.
She sat there watching her husband eat and occasionally taking turns sipping the drink.
Again, the young man came over and begged them to let him buy another meal for
them.
This time, the old woman said 'No, thank you, we are used to sharing everything.'
Finally, as the old man finished and was wiping his face neatly with the napkin,
the young man again came over to the little old lady who had yet to eat a single bite of food and asked
'What is it you are waiting for?'
She answered --
THE TEETH.'

Two eighty year old ladies sat outside the pearly gates. One says 'how did you die?' The other says 'I froze to death' 'that must have been horrible' says the first lady'. 'No', says the second lady, 'after the shivering stopped I felt warm and drowsy and just passed away, anyway, how did you die?' 'I had a heart attack' said the first lady. 'I suspected my husband was having an affair so I came home unexpectedly only to find him watching TV. I went right through the house searching. Checked all the bedrooms, cupboards, wardrobes, under the beds, everywhere but as I came down stairs after all the effort, I had the heart attack'. The second lady said 'you should have checked the freezer, we both would still be alive'.

The great philosopher Lao-Tzu said:
It is only when you see a mosquito land on your testicles that you realise that there are more ways to solve a problem than using violence.

I'm rubbish at French, I can't get past seven.... I think I have a huit allergy.

"I'm worried that those plants are artificial."
"They're not."
"Well that's a real leaf."

An older, white haired man walked into a jewellery store one Friday evening with a beautiful young girl at his side.
He told the jeweller he was looking for a special ring for his girlfriend.
The jeweller looked through his stock and brought out a £5,000 ring and showed it to him.
The old man said, "I don't think you understand, I want something very special."
At that statement, the jeweller went to his special stock and brought another ring over. "Here's a stunning ring at only £40,000," the jeweller said.
The young lady's eyes sparkled and her whole body trembled with excitement.
The old man seeing this said, "We'll take it."
The jeweller asked how payment would be made and the old man stated, "by cheque."
"I know you need to make sure my cheque is good, so I'll write it now and you can call the bank Monday to verify the funds and I'll pick the ring up Monday afternoon."
Monday morning, a very teed-off jeweller phoned the old man. "There's no money in that account."

“I know”, said the old man, “but can you imagine what a weekend I had?”

An old manual has been found at the back of a cupboard in a Dublin second-hand bookshop. The title is:
IRISH DANCING Volume 2 - WHAT TO DO WITH THE HANDS AND ARMS.

A primary school decides to take the Primary 1, 2's and 3's on a field trip to the local racetrack to learn about horses.
When it was time to take the children to the bathroom, it was decided that the girls would go with one teacher and the boys would go with the other.
The teacher assigned to the boys was waiting outside the men’s room when one of the boys came out and told her that none of them could reach the urinals.
Having no choice, she went inside, helped the boys with their pants, and began hoisting the little boys up one by one, holding on to their cocks to get the streamies into the high up urinals and not all over their clothes.
As she lifted one, she couldn't help but notice that he was unusually well endowed. Trying not to show that she was staring the teacher said, 'You must be in Primary 7.'
'Naw, missus', he replied. 'I'm riding Silver Arrow in the fourth but cheers fur yer help.'

According to Tetley, the best way to make a cup of tea is to agitate the bag.
So every morning, I slap her arse and say *"Two sugars fatty!"*

This is my step ladder! I never knew my real ladder.

My wife walked out on me after I blew our entire life savings on a penis extension..
She said she just couldn't take it any longer...

Bob was about to marry Caroline when his father took him to one side.
'When I married your mother, the first thing I did when we got home was take off my trousers,' he said. 'I gave them to your mother and told her to put them on.'
When she did, they were enormous on her and she said to me that she couldn't possibly wear them, as they were too large.
I told her, "Of course they're too big. I wear the trousers in this family and I always will. “Ever since that day, we have never had a single problem.'
Bob took his father's advice and as soon as he got Caroline alone after the wedding, he did the same thing; took off his trousers, gave them to Caroline and told her to put them on.
Caroline said that the trousers were too big and she couldn't possibly wear them. 'Exactly,' replied Bob. 'I wear the trousers in this relationship and I always will. I don't want you to forget that.'
Caroline paused and removed her knickers and gave them to Bob. 'Try these on,' she said, so he tried them on but they were too small. 'I can't possibly get into your knickers,' said Bob.
'Exactly,' replied Caroline. 'And if you don't change your bloody attitude, you never will!'

Sometimes I feel totally useful and nothing I do in this life matters in the slightest - everything I do is pointless.
Then I remember the man who fits indicators to BMW's...

The Smiths were unable to conceive children
and decided to use a surrogate father to start their family.
On the day the proxy father was to arrive,
Mr. Smith kissed his wife goodbye and said,
'Well, I'm off now. The man should be here soon.'

Half an hour later, just by chance, a door-to-door baby photographer happened to ring the doorbell, hoping to make a sale.
'Good morning, Ma'am', he said, 'I've come to...'
'Oh, no need to explain,' Mrs. Smith cut in, embarrassed,
'I've been expecting you.'
'Have you really?' said the photographer.
'Well, that's good. Did you know babies are my specialty?'
'Well that's what my husband and I had hoped.
Please come in and have a seat!.
After a moment she asked, blushing,
'well, where do we start?'
'Leave everything to me. I usually try two in the bathtub,
one on the couch, and perhaps a couple on the bed. And sometimes the living room floor is fun.
You can really spread out there.'
'Bathtub, living room floor?
No wonder it didn't work out for Harry and me!'
'Well, Ma'am, none of us can guarantee a good one every time.
But if we try several different positions
and I shoot from six or seven angles,
I'm sure you'll be pleased with the results.'
'My, that's a lot!', gasped Mrs. Smith.
'Ma'am, in my line of work a man has to take his time.
I'd love to be In and out in five minutes,
but I'm sure you'd be disappointed with that.'
'Don't I know it,' said Mrs. Smith quietly.
The photographer opened his briefcase
and pulled out a portfolio of his baby pictures.
'This was done on the top of a bus,' he said.
'Oh, my God!' Mrs. Smith exclaimed,
grasping at her throat.
'And these twins turned out exceptionally well
- when you consider their mother was so difficult to work with..'
'She was difficult?' asked Mrs. Smith.
'Yes, I'm afraid so. I finally had to take her to the park to get the job done right.
People were crowding around four and five deep to get a good look'
'Four and five deep?' said Mrs. Smith, her eyes wide with amazement.
'Yes', the photographer replied.
'And for more than three hours, too.
The mother was constantly squealing and yelling
- I could hardly concentrate, and when darkness approached I had to rush my shots.

Finally, when the squirrels began nibbling on my equipment, I just had to pack it all in.'
Mrs. Smith leaned forward.
'Do you mean they actually chewed on your, uh...equipment?'
'It's true, Ma'am, yes.
Well, if you're ready, I'll set-up my tripod and we can get to work right away..'
'Tripod?'
'Oh yes, Ma'am. I need to use a tripod to rest my Canon on.
It's much too big to be held in the hand very long.'

Mrs. Smith fainted

A gynaecologist had become fed up with malpractice insurance and paperwork, and was burned out.
Hoping to try another career where skilful
hands would be beneficial, he decided to become a mechanic.
He went to the local technical college, signed up for evening classes, attended diligently, and learned all he could.
When the time of the practical exam approached, the gynaecologist prepared
carefully for weeks, and completed the exam with tremendous skill. When the
results came back, he was surprised to find that he had obtained a score of
150%. Fearing an error, he called the Instructor, saying, "I don't want to appear ungrateful for such an outstanding result, but I wonder if there is an error in the grade?"
"The instructor said, "During the exam, you took the engine apart perfectly,
which was worth 50% of the total mark. You put the engine back together again perfectly, which is also worth 50% of the mark." After a pause, the instructor added, "I gave you an extra 50% because you did it all through the exhaust - which I've never seen done in my entire career."

WOMAN'S DIARY:
Saturday 25th October 2014
Saw him in the evening and he was acting really strangely. I had been shopping in the afternoon with the girls and I did turn up a bit late so thought it might be that.

The bar was really crowded and loud so I suggested we go somewhere quieter to talk. He was still very subdued and distracted so I suggested we go somewhere nice to eat.

All through dinner he just didn't seem himself; he hardly laughed and didn't seem to be paying any attention to me or to what I was saying. I just knew that something was wrong.

He dropped me back home and I wondered if he was going to come in; he hesitated but followed.

I asked him again if there was something the matter but he just half shook his head and turned the television on.

After about 10 minutes of silence, I said I was going upstairs to bed.

I put my arms around him and told him that I loved him deeply. He just gave a sigh and a sad sort of smile. He didn't follow me up but later he did, and I was surprised when we made love.

He still seemed distant and a bit cold, and I started to think that he was going to leave me and that he had found someone else.

I cried myself to sleep.

MANS DIARY:

Saturday 25th October 2014

Leeds lost, Gutted. Got a shag though.

Brummie walks into a tailors...

"Alroit, mate. I'd like a 70s suit, please."

The tailor says, "Certainly sir, and would you like a kipper tie?"

Brummie says, "Thanks mate, two sugars."

Old Israeli man has gone to the Wall in Jerusalem to pray, every day for 60 years.

BBC gets to hear about it and sends out a news team to interview him.

Reporter “Have you really prayed here every day for 60 years?"

Old Man “Yes, twice a day for 60 years and never missed a single day"

Reporter " That is fantastic and what do you pray for?"

Old Man "The same things - peace in the Middle East, and mutual love and understanding with our neighbours. I also pray that my children will grow up prudent and responsible with respect for their elders. Finally, I pray that world leaders will come together in a spirit of understanding and and tolerance so that the world will become a better place.
Reporter" Amazing, and how does it feel?"
"Like talking to a fucking brick wall" was the reply.

"I just deleted all the German names off my phone. It's Hans-free"
"Kim Kardashian is saddled with a huge arse... but enough about Kanye West"
"Surely every car is a people carrier?"
"What's the difference between a 'hippo' and a 'Zippo'? One is really heavy, the other is a little lighter"
"Red sky at night. Shepherd's delight. Blue sky at night. Day"
"Clowns divorce. Custardy battle"

Twenty minutes into an outbound evening flight from Glasgow, the lead flight attendant for the cabin crew nervously makes the following painful announcement..:
"Ladies and gentlemen, I'm so very sorry but it appears that there has been a terrible mix up prior to take off by our airport catering service... I don't know how this has happened but we have 103 passengers on board and, unfortunately, only 40 dinner meals... I truly apologise for this mistake and inconvenience."
When passengers' muttering had died down, she continued, "Anyone who is kind enough to give up their meal so that someone else can eat will receive free, unlimited drinks for the duration of our 5 hour flight."
Her next announcement came 90 minutes later... "If anyone would like to change their minds, we still have 40 dinners available."

A woman was in court charged with assaulting her husband with his guitar collection.
The judge asked "First offender?"
The female defendant replied "No. First a Gibson, then a Fender."

Tom Cruise is to star in a new film about the V.W, exhaust gas scandal. Emission Impassable!

My scouse mate was sending in a loan application today. He said, "I have a good credit history, I think I'll walk it."
"But you're from Liverpool," I said. "You'll never walk a loan."

Apparently there isn't enough crime in my neighbourhood, so guess who'd been asked to go around attacking people in the street?
Yeah, muggins.

A man boarded an airplane and took his seat. As he settled in, he glanced Up and saw the most beautiful woman boarding the plane. He soon realized she was heading straight towards his seat. As fate would have it, she took the seat right beside his. Eager to strike up a conversation he blurted out, “Business trip or pleasure?”
She turned, smiled and said, “Business. I’m going to the Annual Nymphomaniacs of America Convention in Boston."
He swallowed hard. Here was the most gorgeous woman he had ever seen sitting next to him, and she was going to a meeting of nymphomaniacs! Struggling to maintain his composure, he calmly asked, “What’s your Business at this convention?”
“Lecturer,” she responded. “I use information that I have learned from my Personal experiences to debunk some of the popular myths about sexuality.”
“Really?” he said. “And what kind of myths are there?”
“Well,” she explained, “one popular myth is that African-American men are the most well-endowed of all men, when in fact it is the Native American Indian who is most likely to possess that trait. Another popular myth is That Frenchmen are the best lovers, when actually it is Scotsmen who are the best. I have also discovered that the lover with Absolutely the best stamina is the Irish
Suddenly the woman became a little uncomfortable and blushed.. “I’m Sorry,” she said, “I shouldn't really be discussing all of this with you. I don’t even know your name.”
“Tonto,” the man said, “Tonto McTavish but my friends call me Paddy".

A guy goes into the confessional box after years being away from the Catholic Church. He pulls aside the curtain, enters and sits himself down. There's a fully equipped bar with crystal glasses, the best vestry wine, Guinness on tap, cigars and liqueur chocolates nearby, and on the wall a fine photographic display of ladies who appear to have mislaid their garments.

He hears a priest come in: "Father, forgive me for it's been a very long time since I've been to confession and I must admit that the confessional box is much more inviting than it used to be".

The priest replies,

"Get out, you idiot. You're in my side".

I never wanted to believe that my Dad was stealing from his job as a road worker. But when I got home, all the signs were there ...

An elderly Donegal man is stopped by the Gardai around 2am and is asked where he is going at this time of night.

The man replies, "I'm on my way to a lecture about alcohol abuse and the effects it has on the human body, as well as smoking and staying out late."

The Garda officer then asks, "Really? Who is giving that lecture at this time of night?"

The old man replies, "That would be my wife."

99 percent of lawyers give the rest a bad name...

My friends small grandson got lost in Sainsburys.

He approached a uniformed security guard & said I've lost my grandpa

The guard asked "what's he like "

he replied.

Gordon's Gin & women with big breasts

A woman goes to her priest one day and tells him, "Father, I have a problem. I have two female talking parrots, but they only know how to say one thing." "What do they say?" the priest inquired. "They say 'Hi, we're prostitutes. Do you want to have some fun?'" "That's obscene!" the priest exclaimed. Then he thought for a moment. "You know," he said, "I may have a solution to your problem. I have two male talking parrots whom I have taught to pray and read the bible. Bring your two female parrots over to my house, and we'll put them in the cage with Francis and Job. My parrots can teach your parrots to praise and worship, and your parrots are sure to stop saying ...that phrase... in no time." "Thank you," the woman responded, "this may very well be the solution." The next day, she brought her female parrots to the priest's house. As he ushered her in, she saw that his two male parrots were inside their cage, holding rosary beads and praying. Impressed, she walked over and placed her parrots in with them. After a few minutes, the female parrots cried out in unison: "Hi, we're prostitutes. Do you want to have some fun?" There was a stunned silence. Finally, one male parrot looked over at the other male parrot and exclaimed, "Put the beads away, Francis, our prayers have been answered!"

Q. How do you think the unthinkable?
A. With an itheberg.

My girlfriend is getting bored of my obsession with pretending to be a detective, she's suggested we should split up.
It's a good idea, we'll cover more ground that way.

A foreigner was touring the USA on holiday and stopped in a remote bar in the hills of Nevada. He was chatting to the bartender when he spied an old Indian sitting in the corner. He had tribal gear on, long white plaits, wrinkled face. “Who’s he?” said the foreigner.
“That’s the Memory Man.” said the bartender. “He knows everything. He can remember any fact. Go and try him out.”
So the foreigner goes over, and thinking he won’t know about English football, asks “Who won the 1965 FA Cup Final?”

“Liverpool,” replies the Memory Man.
“Who did they beat?”
“Leeds,” was the reply.
“And the score?”
“2-1.”
“Who scored the winning goal?”
“Ian St. John,” was the old man’s reply.
The foreigner was knocked out by this and told everyone back home about the Memory Man when he returned.
A few years later he went back to the USA and tried to find the impressive Memory Man. Eventually he found the bar and sitting in the same seat was the old Indian only this time he was older and more wrinkled. Because he was so impressed, the foreigner decided to greet the Indian in his native tongue.
He approached him with the greeting “How”.
The Memory man replied, “Diving header in the six yard box!!

When I couldn't remember what 51, 6 and 500 were in Roman numerals I was LIVID...

My friend Gavin died yesterday from taking heart burn tablets.
I can't believe Gavisgon...

A busker came up to us the other day & played us a lovely song. Smiling, I asked if he did requests
"sure" he replied
"good, then piss off"

Little Johnny attended a horse auction with his father. He watched as his father moved from horse to horse, slowly running his hands up and down the horses legs and rump, and chest.
After a few minutes, Johnny asked, *"Dad, why are you doing that?"*
His father replied, *"Because when I am buying horses, I have to make*

sure that they are healthy and in absolutely good shape before I buy."
Johnny, looking worried, said, *"Dad .... dad ... I think the Milkman wants to buy Mummy."*

Sex is like playing bridge. If you don't have a good partner, you better have a good hand

3 drunk guys entered a taxi. The taxi driver knew that they were really drunk so he started the engine & turned it off again. Then said,
"We have reached your destination".
The 1st guy gave him money & the 2nd guy said *"Thank you".*
However, the 3rd guy slapped the driver. The driver was shocked thinking the 3rd drunk must have known what he had done and how was he to get out this one.... But then he timidly asked *"What was that for?"*. The 3rd guy replied, *"Control your speed next time, you nearly killed us!"*

Christmas day is on a Friday this year - hope it's not the 13th.

A new business was opening, and one of the owner's friends sent flowers for the occasion. But when the owner read the card with the flowers, it said "Rest in Peace".
The owner was little upset and called the florist to complain. After he had told the florist about the obvious mistake, the florist said, "Sir, I'm really sorry for the mistake, but rather than getting angry, you should imagine this: Somewhere there is a funeral taking place today, and they have flowers with a note saying, "Congratulations on your new location."

A lawyer went duck hunting for the first time in Texas. He shot and dropped a bird, but it fell into a farmer's field on the other side of the fence. As the lawyer climbed over the fence, an elderly farmer drove up on his tractor and asked him what he was doing.
The litigator responded, "I shot a duck, it fell into this field, and now I'm going to retrieve it."
The old farmer replied, "This is my property and you are not coming over here."
The indignant lawyer said, "I am one of the best trial attorneys in the U.S. and if you don't let me get that duck, I'll sue you and take everything you own."

The old farmer smiled and said, "Apparently, you don't know how we do things in Texas. We settle small disagreements like this with the Texas Three-Kick Rule."
The lawyer asked, "What is the Texas Three-Kick Rule?"
The Farmer replied, "Well, first I kick you three times and then you kick me three times, and so on, back and forth, until someone gives up." The attorney quickly thought about the proposed contest and decided that he could easily take the old codger. He agreed to abide by the local custom. The old farmer slowly climbed down from the tractor and walked up to the city feller. His first kick planted the toe of his heavy work boot into the lawyer's groin and dropped him to his knees. His second kick nearly wiped the man's nose off his face. The barrister was flat on his belly when the farmer's third kick to a kidney nearly caused him to give up. The lawyer summoned every bit of his will and managed to get to his feet and said, "Okay, you old coot! Now, it's my turn!"
The old farmer smiled and said, "No, I give up. You can have the duck."

A New York attorney representing a wealthy art collector called and asked to speak to his client, "Saul, I have some good news and, I have some bad news."
The art collector replied, "I've had an awful day; let's hear the good news first."
The lawyer said, "Well, I met with your wife today, and she informed me that she invested $5,000 in two pictures that she thinks will bring a minimum of $15-20 million. I think she could be right."
Saul replied enthusiastically, "Well done! My wife is a brilliant businesswoman! You've just made my day. Now I know I can handle the bad news. What is it?"
The lawyer replied, "The pictures are of you with your secretary."

The Grim Reaper came for me last night, and I beat him off with a vacuum cleaner. Talk about Dyson with death.

A mate of mine recently admitted to being addicted to brake fluid. When I quizzed him on it he reckoned he could stop any time....

I went to the cemetery yesterday to lay some flowers on a grave. As I was standing there I noticed 4 grave diggers walking about with a coffin, 3 hours later and they're still walking about with it. I thought to myself, they've lost the plot!!

I was at an ATM yesterday when a little old lady asked if I could check her balance, so I pushed her over.

I start a new job in Seoul next week. I thought it was a good Korea move.

I was driving this morning when I saw an AA van parked up. The driver was sobbing uncontrollably and looked very miserable. I thought to myself that guy's heading for a breakdown.

Paddy says "Mick, I'm thinking of buying a Labrador ." Sod that" says Mick "have you seen how many of their owners go blind?"

Man calls 999 and says "I think my wife is dead" The operator says how do you know? He says "The sex is the same but the ironing is building up!"

I woke up last night to find the ghost of Gloria Gaynor standing at the foot of my bed. At first I was afraid.......then I was petrified.

A wife says to her husband you're always pushing me around and talking behind my back. He says what do you expect? You're in a wheelchair.

I was explaining to my wife last night that when you die you get reincarnated but must come back as a different creature. She said I would like to come back as a cow. I said you're obviously not listening.

The wife has been missing a week now. Police said to prepare for the worst. So I have been to the charity shop to get all her clothes back.

The wife was counting all the 1p's and 2p's out on the kitchen table when she suddenly got very angry and started shouting and crying for no reason. I thought to myself, "She's going through the change."

Local Police hunting the 'knitting needle nutter', who has stabbed six people in the village in the last 48 hours, believe the attacker could be following some kind of pattern.

A teddy bear is working on a building site. He goes for a tea break and when he returns he notices his pick has been stolen. The bear is angry and reports the theft to the foreman. The foreman grins at the bear and says "Oh, I forgot to tell you, today's the day the teddy bears have their picks nicked.

I thought my wife was joking when she said she wanted to go to a Monkees' concert in Switzerland.
Then I saw her face, now I'm in Geneva.

I see the man suing Ryan air over his missing luggage has lost his case.

Chris Eubanks just finished his first book on ethics. If it sells well the next two books will be on Surrey & Lancashire.

Four well to do English gents go deer stalking in the highlands and get dropped off by helicopter in a remote glen. The pilot says he'll be back in eight hours and bids them a good days shooting.
later the helicopter returns and the gents proudly sporting a Stag each.

The pilot somewhat flummoxed says 'hold on, I can't take you lot and the stags as well'
The gent's all remonstrate that they had bagged the exact same number the previous year and the pilot said it wouldn't be a problem.
'Well, I suppose Ok then if he managed it so should I. But it'll be a tight squeeze' says the pilot
The helicopter sluggishly limbers skyward but after a short while gravity wins and the overladen copter plummets out of the sky.
All five manage to extract themselves from the tangled wreckage with no more than cuts an bruises and the Pilot asks 'Where the fuck are we?'
The gent's have a quick glance around and say to the pilot 'The same place we crashed last year'

A tourist in Vienna is going through a graveyard and all of a sudden he hears music.
No one is around, so he starts searching for the source.
He finally locates the origin and finds it is coming from a grave with a headstone that
reads "Ludwig van Beethoven, 1770- 1827".
Then he realizes that the music is the Ninth Symphony and it is being played backward!
Puzzled, he leaves the graveyard and persuades a friend to return with him.
By the time they arrive back at the grave, the music has changed.
This time it is the Seventh Symphony, but like the previous piece, it is being played backward.
Curious, the men agree to consult a music scholar.
When they return with the expert, the Fifth Symphony is playing, again backward.
The expert notices that the symphonies are being played in the reverse order in which they were composed,
the 9th, then the 7th, then the 5th.
By the next day the word has spread and a crowd has gathered around the grave.
They are all listening to the Second Symphony being played backward.
Just then the graveyard's caretaker ambles up to the group.
Someone in the group asks him if he has an explanation for the music.
"I would have thought it was obvious" the caretaker says.
"He's decomposing."

A Member of Parliament to Disraeli: "Sir, you will either die on the gallows or of some unspeakable disease."

"That depends, Sir," said Disraeli, "whether I embrace your policies or your mistress."

"He had delusions of adequacy." - Walter Kerr

"He has all the virtues I dislike and none of the vices I admire." - Winston Churchill

"I have never killed a man, but I have read many obituaries with great pleasure." Clarence Darrow

"He has never been known to use a word that might send a reader to the dictionary." - William Faulkner (about Ernest Hemingway).

"Thank you for sending me a copy of your book; I'll waste no time reading it." - Moses Hadas

"I didn't attend the funeral, but I sent a nice letter saying I approved of it." - Mark Twain

"He has no enemies, but is intensely disliked by his friends." - Oscar Wilde

"I am enclosing two tickets to the first night of my new play; bring a friend, if you have one." - George Bernard Shaw to Winston Churchill.

"Cannot possibly attend first night, will attend second ... if there is one." - Winston Churchill, in response.

"I feel so miserable without you; it's almost like having you here." - Stephen Bishop

"He is a self-made man and worships his creator." - John Bright

"I've just learned about his illness. Let's hope it's nothing trivial." - Irvin S. Cobb

"He is not only dull himself; he is the cause of dullness in others." - Samuel Johnson

"He is simply a shiver looking for a spine to run up." - Paul Keating

"In order to avoid being called a flirt, she always yielded easily." -

Charles, Count Talleyrand
"He loves nature in spite of what it did to him." - Forrest Tucker
"Why do you sit there looking like an envelope without any address on it?" - Mark Twain
"His mother should have thrown him away and kept the stork." - Mae West
"Some cause happiness wherever they go; others, whenever they go."- Oscar Wilde
"He uses statistics as a drunken man uses lamp-posts... for support rather than illumination." - Andrew Lang (1844-1912)
"He has Van Gogh's ear for music." - Billy Wilder
"I've had a perfectly wonderful evening. But this wasn't it." - Groucho Marx

I'm not saying my wife is ugly but a peeping tom knocked on my door last night and asked me to close the curtains!

Got home, entered the front door, and found the wife crying, I said, "What's the matter, dear?" - I always call her 'dear', on account on her expensive tastes.
She said, "I'm homesick!"
I said, "What do you mean, homesick? But this is your home!"
She said, "I know! I'm sick of it!"

-As I walked out of the front door with my bags last night, I looked back at my wife and said, "Are you sure about this? It doesn't feel right."
"Yes, I'm sure," she replied. "You're a lazy bastard and it's about time."
"What about the kids?" I asked.
"They're busy watching TV," she said. "Now just be a man, for once, and put the rubbish out."

The police came to my front door last night holding a picture of my wife. They said "is this your wife sir?". Shocked I answered “yes".
They said "I'm afraid it looks like she's been hit by a bus".
I said "I know, but she has a lovely personality"

Lionel Messi goes up to a hot girl in a bar and says "Get your coat, you've pulled",
she replied ... "Wow, you're a little forward"

Bob Marley's wife has left him and she's taken the satelite dish with her.
What a bastard!!!!!
No woman, no sky.

Captain "I didn't see you at camouflage training this morning private Murphy!" Murphy "Thank you sir!"

Why did Adele cross the road?
So she could say "hello" from the other side!

Three submariners died on Christmas Eve and were met by Saint Peter at the pearly gates.
'In honour of this holy season' Saint Peter said, 'You must each possess something that symbolises Christmas to get into heaven.'
The Englishman fumbled through his pockets and pulled out a lighter. He flicked it on. 'It's a candle', he said.
'You may pass through the pearly gates' Saint Peter said.
The Canadian reached into his pocket and pulled out a set of keys. He shook them and said, 'They're bells.'
Saint Peter said 'You may pass through the pearly gates'.
The Australian started searching desperately through his pockets and finally pulled out a pair of women's panties.
St. Peter looked at the man with a raised eyebrow and asked, 'and just what do those symbolise?'
The Australian replied, 'These are Carols.'

An elderly Irish woman of advanced age visited her doctor to ask his advice on reviving her husband's lagging libido.
'What about trying Viagra?" asked the doctor.
"Not a chance," she said... *"He won't even take an aspirin."*
"Not a problem," replied the doctor. *"Give him an "Irish Viagra."*
"What's an Irish Viagra?" she asked.

"You drop the Viagra tablet into his coffee. He won't even taste it. Give it a try and call me in a week to let me know how things went."
A week later she called the doctor, who asked her about the results.
"Oh, faith, bejaysus and begorrah!" she exclaimed. *"T'was horrid! Just terrible, doctor!"*
"Really? What happened?" asked the doctor.
"Well, I did as you advised and slipped it in his coffee and the effect was immediate.
He jumped straight up, with a twinkle in his eye! With one swoop of his arm, he sent cups and tablecloth flying, then ripped me clothes to tatters and took me then and there on the tabletop! T'was a nightmare, I tell you, an absolute nightmare!"
"Why so terrible?" asked the doctor, *"Do you mean it wasn't good?"*
"It was the best I've had in 25 years! But sure as I'm sittin' here, I'll never be able to show me face in Starbucks again!"

My mate is in hospital after eating a dodgy curry.
The buggers, instead of using proper veg, they mixed in some daffodil bulbs.
Poor lad isn't due out until spring.

A man walks into a bar with a newt on his shoulder.
The barman says that's a nice newt, what's its name?
The man says Tiny.
The barman asks why do you call it Tiny.
The man say, because it's my newt...

As a trucker stops for a red light, a blonde catches up. She jumps out of her car, runs up to his truck, and knocks on the door. The trucker lowers the window, and she says "Hi, my name is Heather and you are losing some of your load." The trucker ignores her and proceeds down the street. When the truck stops for another red light, the girl catches up again. She jumps out of her car, runs up and knocks on the door. Again, the trucker lowers the window. As if they've never spoken, the blonde says brightly, "Hi my name is Heather, and you are losing some of your load!" Shaking his head, the trucker ignores her again and continues down the street. At the third red light, the same thing happens again. All out of breath, the blonde gets out of her car, runs up, knocks on the truck door. The trucker lowers the window. Again she says "Hi, my name is Heather, and you are losing some of your load!" When the light turns green the trucker revs up and races to the next light. When he stops this time, he hurriedly gets out of the truck, and runs back to the blonde. He knocks on her window, and as she lowers it, he says "Hi, my name is Kevin, it's winter in Canada and I'm driving the SALT TRUCK!"

A successful rancher died and left everything to his devoted wife.
She was a very good-looking woman and determined to keep the ranch, but knew very little about ranching, so she decided to place an ad in the newspaper for a ranch hand...
Two cowboys applied for the job. One was gay and the other a drunk.
She thought long and hard about it, and when no one else applied she decided to hire the gay guy, figuring it would be safer to have him around the house than the drunk.
He proved to be a hard worker who put in long hours every day and knew a lot about ranching..
For weeks, the two of them worked, and the ranch was doing very well.
Then one day, the rancher's widow said to the hired hand, "You have done a really good job, and the ranch looks great. You should go into town and kick up your heels." The hired hand readily agreed and went into town one Saturday night.
One o'clock came, however, and he didn't return.
Two o'clock and no hired hand.
Finally he returned around two-thirty, and upon entering the room, he found the rancher's widow sitting by the fireplace with a glass of wine, waiting for him.
She quietly called him over to her..
"Unbutton my blouse and take it off," she said.
Trembling, he did as she directed. "Now take off my boots."
He did as she asked, ever so slowly. "Now take off my socks."
He removed each gently and placed them neatly by her boots.
"Now take off my skirt."
He slowly unbuttoned it, constantly watching her eyes in the fire light.
"Now take off my bra.." Again, with trembling hands, he did as he was told and dropped it to the floor.
Then she looked at him and said, "If you ever wear my clothes into town again, you're fired."

One year, I decided to buy my mother-in-law a cemetery plot as a Christmas gift...

The next year, I didn't buy her a gift.
When she asked me why, I replied, "Well, you still haven't used the gift I bought you last year!"
And that's how the fight started.....

I took my wife to a restaurant.
The waiter, for some reason, took my order first.
"I'll have the rump steak, rare, please."
He said, "Aren't you worried about the mad cow?"
"Nah, she can order for herself."
And that's when the fight started.....

My wife sat down next to me as I was flipping channels
she asked, "What's on TV?"
I said, "Dust."
And that's when the fight started.

After retiring, I went to the Social Security office to apply for Social Security.
The woman behind the counter asked me for my driver's license to verify my age.
I looked in my pockets and realized I had left my wallet at home. I told the woman that I was very sorry, but I would have to go home and come back later.
The woman said, 'Unbutton your shirt'.
So I opened my shirt revealing my curly silver hair.
She said, 'That silver hair on your chest is proof enough for me' and she processed my Social Security application.
When I got home, I excitedly told my wife about my experience at the Social Security office.
She said, 'You should have dropped your pants. You might have gotten disability too.'
And that's when the fight started...

I rear-ended a car this morning...the start of a REALLY bad day!
The driver got out of the other car, and he was a DWARF!!
He looked up at me and said 'I am NOT Happy!'
So I said, 'Well, which one ARE you then?'
And that's when the fight started.

Daddy, why do people hang horses?" asked my daughter.
"Nobody hangs horses, darling," As I consoled her. "Who told you that people hang horses?"
"No-one, - I just heard mummy on the phone saying that her new boss was hung like a horse."

Englishman, Irishman and Scotsman in a psychology lesson.
Teacher asks Englishman what's opposite of joy? He says sorrow.
He asks Scotsman what's opposite of depression? He says happiness.
He asks, Paddy what's the opposite of woe? He says.....giddy up!

Through the pitch-black night, the captain sees a light dead ahead on a collision course with his ship. He sends a signal: "Change your course ten degrees east." The light signals back: "Change yours, ten degrees west."
Angry, the captain sends: "I'm a Navy captain! Change your course, sir!"
"I'm a seaman, second class," comes the reply. "Change your course, sir."
Now the captain is furious. "I'm a battleship! I'm not changing course!"
There's one last reply. "I'm a lighthouse. Your call."

A man walks into a restaurant with a full-grown ostrich behind him. The waitress asks them for their orders. The man says, "A hamburger, fries and a coke," and turns to the ostrich, "What'syours?" "I'll have the same," says the ostrich.
A short time later the waitress returns with the order. "That will Be £9.40 please" The man reaches into his pocket and pulls out the exact change for payment.
The next day, the man and the ostrich come again and the man says, "A hamburger, fries and a coke."
The ostrich says, "I'll have the same."

Again the man reaches into his pocket and pays with exact change. This becomes routine until the two enter again. "The usual?" Asks the waitress. "No, this is Friday night, so I will have a steak, baked potato and a salad," says the man. "Same," says the ostrich. Shortly the waitress brings the order and says, "That will be £32.62." Once again the man pulls the exact change out of his pocket and places it on the table.
The waitress cannot hold back her curiosity any longer. "Excuse me, Sir. How do you manage to always come up with the exact change in your pocket every time?"
"Well," says the man, "several years ago I was cleaning the attic and Found an old lamp. When I rubbed it, a Genie appeared and offered me two wishes. My first wish was that if I ever had to pay for anything, I would just put my hand in my pocket and the right amount of money would always be there."
"That's brilliant!" says the waitress. "Most people would ask for a Million Dollars or something, but you'll always be as rich as you want for as long as you live!"
"That's right. Whether it's a gallon of milk or a Rolls Royce, the exact money is always there," says the man.
The waitress asks, "What's with the ostrich?"
The man sighs, pauses and answers, "My second wish was for a tall bird with long legs who agrees with everything I say"

This blonde wanted to sell her pet Python so, she listed it on eBay.
A bloke rang up and asked if it was big.
She said, "It's really massive."
He said, "Ah, how many feet then?"
She said - "Are you thick or what? It's a bloody Snake"!!

A woman phoned her blond male neighbour and said:
"Close your curtains the next time you and your wife are having sex. The whole street was watching and laughing at YOU yesterday."
To which the blond man replied:
"Well the joke's on "ALL OF YOU" because I wasn't even at home yesterday!

Frank and his mates had a novel idea, they were all keen climbers and poker players. One long weekend they climbed 2000 feet, played a game of poker and cooked themselves a bit of rump, and the next day they made it to 4000 feet, played another game and cooked themselves a bit of sirloin. The following day they got to 6000 feet played another game and had some silverside.
At 8000 feet after losing a bit of money Frank decided to quit. His disappointed mates asked why and Frank explained "the steaks are too high".

His request approved, the CNN News photographer quickly used a cell phone to call the local airport to charter a flight.
He was told a twin-engine plane would be waiting for him at the airport.
Arriving at the airfield, he spotted a plane warming up outside a hanger.
He jumped in with his bag, slammed the door shut, and shouted, 'Let's go'.
The pilot taxied out, swung the plane into the wind and took off.
Once in the air, the photographer instructed the pilot, 'Fly over the valley and make low passes so I can take pictures of the fires on the hillsides.'
'Why?' asked the pilot.
'Because I'm a photographer for CNN', he responded, 'and I need to get some close up shots.'
The pilot was strangely silent for a moment, finally he stammered, 'So, what you're telling me, is . . . You're NOT my flight instructor?'

A man walks into a zoo. The only animal in the zoo is a dog.
It was a shitzu.

I've decided to sell my Hoover... well it was just collecting dust.
I heard a rumour that Cadbury is bringing out an oriental chocolate bar.
Could be a Chinese Wispa.

Crime in multi-storey car parks. That is wrong on so many different levels.

An elderly Bosnian man who lived on the outskirts of Sarajevo went to his local church for confession. When the priest slid open the panel in the confessional box, the man said:
"Father, during the Balkan war in the 90s, an incredibly beautiful young Slav woman from our neighbourhood knocked urgently on my door and asked me to hide her from the Serbian militia. So I hid her in my attic."
The priest replied: *"That was a wonderful thing you did, and you have no need to confess that."*
The man continued: *"There is more to tell, Father. She started to repay me with sexual favours. This happened several times a week, and sometimes twice on Sundays."*
The priest said, *"That was quite a long time ago and by doing what you did, you placed the two of you in great danger, but two people under those circumstances can easily succumb to the weakness of the flesh. However, if you are truly sorry for your actions, you are indeed forgiven."*
"Thank you, Father. That's a great load off my mind. I do have one more question."
"And what is that?" asked the priest.......
"Should I tell her the war is over ?"

Went to the doctors with hearing problems. He said "Can you describe the symptoms?"
I said "Homer's fat and Marge has blue hair"

A bus stops and 2 Italian men get on. They sit down and
engage in an animated conversation.
The lady sitting next to them ignores them at first, but
her attention is galvanized when she hears one of them say the following:
'Emma come first.
Den I come.
Den two asses come together.
I come once-a-more !
Two asses, they come together again.
I come again and pee twice.
Then I come one lasta time.'

The lady can't take this anymore,
'You foul-mouthed sex obsessed pig !' she retorted indignantly. 'In this country, we don't speak aloud in Public places about our sex lives!'
'Hey, coola down lady,' said the man. 'Who talkin' bouta sex? I'm a justa tellin' my frienda how to spell 'Mississippi.'

A pretty little girl named Suzy was sitting on the pavement in front of her home.
Next to her was a basket containing a number of tiny creatures; in her hand was a sign announcing “FREE KITTENS.”
Suddenly a line of big cars pulled up beside her.
Out of the lead car stepped a grinning man. “Hi there little girl, I'm the leader of the Conservative Party, David Cameron, what do you have in the basket?” he asked.
“Kittens,” little Suzy said. “How old are they?” asked Mr Cameron. Suzy replied, “They're so young, their eyes aren't even open yet.”
“And what kind of kittens are they?” “They're REMAIN IN THE EU supporters,” answered Suzy with a sweet smile.
Mr Cameron was delighted, a golden opportunity beckoned.
As soon as he returned to his car, he called his PR chief and told him about the little girl and the kittens.
Recognizing the perfect photo op, the three of them agreed that they should return the next day; and in front of the assembled media, have the girl talk about her discerning kittens.
So the next day, Suzy was again on the pavement with her basket of “FREE KITTENS,” when Cameron's motorcade pulled up, this time followed by vans from BBC, ITV, Channels 4, Channels 5, CNN and Sky News.
Cameras and the audio equipment were quickly set up, then Cameron got out of his limo and walked over to little Suzy. “Hello, again,” he said, “I'd love it if you would tell all my friends out there what kind of kittens you're giving away.”
“Yes sir,” Suzy said. “They're BREXIT supporters.”
Taken by surprise, David Cameron stammered, “But yesterday, you told me they were REMAIN IN THE EU SUPPORTERS.”
Little Suzy smiled and said, “I know. But today, they have their eyes open.”

A very pretty young speech therapist with an equally fine figure was getting absolutely nowhere with her Stammer's Action Group. She had tried virtually every technique in the book, but still they stammered and stuttered.

Finally, totally exasperated, she said: *"If any of you can tell me where you were born,*

without stuttering, I will have wild and passionate sex with you until your muscles ache

and your eyeswater."

The Englishman immediately piped up: *"B-b-b-b-b-b-b-irmingham"*, he said.

"That's no use, Trevor" said the speech therapist, *"Who's going to try next?"*

The Scotsman raised his hand and blurted out: "G-g-g-g-g-g-gl-lasgow".

"That's no better either, Hamish. ... Now, how about you, Paddy?"

The Irishman took a deep breath, counted to 5, clenched both fists at his sides and

eventually blurted out:. . . . . *"London "*.

"Absolutely Brilliant, Paddy!" said the speech therapist and immediately set about living up to her promise. After 15 minutes of exceptionally hot and steamy sex, the couple paused for breath and Paddy said: "d-d-d-d-d-d-d-d-d-d-d-erry".

An old teacher asked her student, "If I say, 'I am beautiful,' which tense is that?"

The student replied, "It is obviously past."

I once built a nuclear missile silo in my back garden.

My wife went ballistic.

Three sisters ages 92, 94 and 96 live in a house together.

One night the 96 year old draws a bath. She puts her foot in and pauses.

She yells to the other sisters, "Was I getting in or out of the bath?"

The 94 year old yells back "I don't know. I'll come up and see."

She starts up the stairs and pauses "Was I going up the stairs or down?"
The 92 year old is sitting at the kitchen table having tea listening to her sisters.
She shakes her head and says, "I sure hope I never get that forgetful." She knocks on wood for good measure. She then yells, "I'll come up and help both of you as soon as I see who's at the door."

God asked, "What is it, Eve?"
Eve replied, "I know that you created me and provided this beautiful garden and all these wonderful animals, especially that hilarious snake, but I'm just not happy."
"And why is that Eve?"
"Lord, I'm lonely, and I'm sick to death of apples."
"Well, Eve, in that case I have a solution. I shall create a man for you."
"Man? What is that Lord?"
"A flawed creature with many bad traits. He'll lie, cheat and be vain. All in all, he'll give you a hard time, but he'll be bigger and faster and will love to hunt, fish, and bring you good things to eat. I'll create him in such a way that he will satisfy your physical needs. He will be witless and will revel in childish things like playing cards and gambling and knocking a ball around. He won't be as smart as you, so he will also need your advice to think properly."
"Sounds great," said Eve, with ironically raised eyebrows, "but what's the catch?"
"Well,.. you can have him on one condition."
"And what's that, Lord?"

"Well, since he'll be proud, arrogant, and self-admiring, you'll have to let him believe that I made him first. And it will have to be our secret ... you know, woman to woman."

A woman came home, screeching her car into the driveway, and ran into the house. She slammed the door and shouted at the top of her lungs, 'Honey, pack your bags. I won the lottery!' The husband said, 'Oh my God! What should I pack, beach stuff or mountain stuff?' 'Doesn't matter,' she said. 'Just get out.'

Marriage is a relationship in which one person is always right, and the other is a husband.

Mother Superior called all the nuns together and said to them, 'I must tell you all something. We have a case of gonorrhoea in the convent.' 'Thank God,' said an elderly nun at the back. 'I'm so tired of chardonnay.'

Fifty-one years ago, Herman James, a North Carolina mountain man, was drafted by the Army. On his first day in basic training, the Army issued him a comb that afternoon the Army barber sheared off all his hair. On his second day, the Army issued Herman a toothbrush. That afternoon the Army dentist yanked seven of his teeth. On the third day, the Army issued him a jock strap. The Army has been looking for Herman for 51 years.

My Doctor just gave me a prescription for daily sex....
however my wife insists it's for ... **dyslexia** !!

Her indoors and I went to the local farmers show and one of the first exhibits we stopped at was the breeding bulls. We went up to the first pen and there was a sign attached that said,
' THIS BULL MATED 50 TIMES LAST YEAR'
She playfully nudged me in the ribs .....Smiled and said, 'He mated 50 times last year.'
We walked to the second pen which had a sign attached that said,
"THIS BULL MATED 150 TIMES LAST YEAR'
She again gave me a healthy jab and said, 'WOW~~That's more than twice a week! ....You could learn a lot from him.'
We walked to the third pen and it had a sign attached that said,
in capital letters,
'THIS BULL MATED 365 TIMES LAST YEAR'
She was so excited that her elbow nearly broke my ribs, and said,
'That's once a day ..You could REALLY learn something from this one.'
I looked at her and said,
"Go over and ask him if it was the same old cow he shagged every time?"

I went to the zoo yesterday and can you believe, I saw eight large baguettes in a cage.
The zoo keeper told me they were bread in captivity...

Bloke goes to Lord's for the Test match, England v Australia.
Next to him is an old man who appears to be on his own, and then an empty seat. Curious as to why a game that sold out months ago has an empty seat, he asks the old man if someone is joining him.
"No", says the old boy. "That was supposed to be my wife's seat, but she's passed away. We came to every Test match here for 20 years, and these were always our seats. This is the first time I've come without her."
"Oh, I'm sorry" says the man. Then he thinks and says "But couldn't you have brought a friend or family member with you instead?"
"Oh no," says the old man. "They're all at the funeral."

My Chinese neighbour said that he's just opened a crows shop, I said "don't you mean a clothes shop?"
He says no a crows shop.
I said "OK I'll have to swing by and have a rook".

So what if I don't know what apocalypse means!?
It's not the end of the world!

A Guy stuck his head into a barbershop and asked, 'How long before I can get a haircut?
The barber looked around the shop full of customers and said, 'About 2 hours.'
The guy left.
A few days later, the same guy stuck his head in the door and asked, 'How long before I can get a haircut?'
The barber looked around at the shop and said, 'About 3 hours.'
The guy left.
A week later, the same guy stuck his head in the shop and asked, 'How long before I can get a haircut?'
The barber looked around the shop and said, 'About an hour and a half.
The guy left.
The barber turned to his friend and said, 'Hey, Bob, do me a favour, follow him and see where he goes. He keeps asking how long he has to wait for a haircut, but he never comes back.'
A little while later, Bob returned to the shop, laughing hysterically.
The barber asked, 'So, where does he go when he leaves?'
Bob looked up, wiped the tears from his eyes and said....

'Your house.

Someone threw a bottle of omega 3 pills at me the other day......
luckily my injuries were only super fish oil

Apparently white bears have a disorder that means that they have sex with both female and male white bears.
Scientists have discovered that they are Bi-polar.

A shepherd sent his sheepdog out to gather and count the flock to make sure none were missing.
The dog returned and says that there are 100 sheep.
The shepherd says, "100? I only started with 97".
The dog replies, "Yeah, but you told me to round them up".

A man asked an American Indian what was his wife's name.
He replied: "She is called Five Horses".
The man said: "That's an unusual name for your wife.
What does it mean?"
The old Indian replied:
"It old Indian name. It mean ...
NAG, NAG, NAG, NAG, NAG

Husband takes the wife to a nightclub. There's a guy on the dance floor giving it big licks - break dancing, moon walking, back flips, the works. The wife turns to her husband and says: "See that guy? 25 years ago he proposed to me and I turned him down." Husband says: "Looks like he's still celebrating!!"

My mate just got barred from B&Q, some guy in an orange apron came up to him and asked if he wanted decking, luckily he got the first punch in !!

An Englishman an Irishman and a Scotsman where painting the Forth Bridge and at lunch time they all sat down together on a beam high above the Firth of Forth. The Englishman opened his lunch box, rolled his eyes and cursed saying "fucking cheese and ham sandwiches again, I told her last week I liked cheese and ham and that's all I bloody get now" he continued "If I get cheese and ham again tomorrow I'll jump of this fucking bridge!"

The Scotsman then opened his lunchbox and declared "for feck sake it, fuckin egg and onion again, is that all my missus knows how to make, I'm with you pal, if get egg and onion again tomorrow I'm off the bridge as well.

Paddy then opened his box and cried out "oh my god, feck me, chicken and mayo again" he shook his head and looked at his mates. "If I get chicken and mayo tomorrow I'm fucking jumping too.

The next day at lunch the Englishman opens his lunchbox and can't believe it, there's an apple a biscuit and packet of crisps.

The Scottish fella opens his lunch and smiles, there inside is a lovely salad with bacon bits and a stick dressing.

Paddy opens his box looks at his mates, he starts to shake as there in the box are 2 chicken and mayo sandwiches. Without a word Paddy stands up and steps off the bridge and disappears into the frigid water far below.

Several days later at the funeral Paddy's mates were comforting his wife explaining the agreement they had come too. "But I don't understand" she eventually manages through sobs "Paddy always made his own lunches !"

Jokes about white sugar are rare... Jokes about brown sugar.. Dem are rarer

I got me and the Mrs a water bed a while back but we had to get rid of it we were drifting apart

Upon hearing that her elderly grandfather had just passed away, Katie went straight to her grandparent's house to visit her 95 year-old grandmother and comfort her.

When she asked how her grandfather had died, her grandmother replied *"He had a heart attack while we were making love on Sunday morning."*

Horrified, Katie told her grandmother that 2 people nearly 100 years old having sex would surely be asking for trouble.

"Oh no, my dear," replied granny.

"Many years ago, realizing our advanced age, we figured out the best time to do it was when the church bells would start to ring. It was just the right rhythm. Nice and slow and even. Nothing too strenuous, simply in on the Ding and out on the Dong."

She paused to wipe away a tear, and continued, *"He'd still be alive if the ice cream van hadn't come along."*

The Lone Ranger was captured by an enemy Indian war party. The Indian chief proclaims so you are the famous Lone Ranger. In honour of the harvest festival you will be killed in 3 days. Before I have you killed I will grant you 3 requests, what is your first request. The Lone Ranger says I'd like to speak to my horse Silver.

The Chief nods and Silver is brought before the Lone Ranger who whispers in Silver's ear, and the horse gallops away.

Later that evening, Silver returns with a beautiful blonde woman on his back.

As the Indian Chief watches, the blonde enters the Lone Ranger's tent and spends the night.
The next morning the Indian Chief admits he's impressed.
"You have a very fine and loyal horse",
"But I will still kill you in two days."
"What is your SECOND request?"
The Lone Ranger again asks to speak to his horse. Silver is brought to him, and he again whispers in the horse's ear. As before, Silver takes off and disappears over the horizon.
Later that evening, to the Chief's surprise, Silver again returns,
this time with a voluptuous brunette, more attractive than the blonde.
She enters the Lone Rangers tent and spends the night. The following morning the Indian Chief is again impressed. "You are indeed a man of many talents,"
"But I will still kill you tomorrow." "What is your LAST request?"
The Lone Ranger responds, "I'd like to speak to my horse...alone."
The Chief is curious, but he agrees, and Silver is brought to
the Lone Ranger's tent. Once they're alone, the Lone Ranger grabs Silver by both ears,
looks him square in the eye and says,

"Listen Very Carefully!!!
FOR...THE...LAST...TIME...
"BRING POSSE!!
If easily offended skip this

Sammy and Agnes are in their 90s and both live in a home. Sammy had only arrived a fortnight earlier when at dinner Agnes says to him "Sammy why don't you grow a set and ask me out, you've been looking at me since you arrived."
Sammy was a tad taken aback but did admit that he thought she was a good looking woman.

"Ok," said Agnes "then come to my room at 10pm tonight."

Later that night around 8:30pm Sammy set off for Agnes's room and arrived just on 10pm, he rang the doorbell and Agnes answered the door wearing very little, "come on in" she urged Sammy.

Sammy went in and was about to sit down on the sofa when Agnes said, "what are you doing sitting down, we haven't got much time left get into the bedroom."

Sammy did just as he was told and Agnes joined him, slipping into the bed and demanding he joined her.

Once in Agnes asked him what his preference in sex was. Being a gentlemen he said "why don't you choose" to which she replied "well I have always enjoyed oral so get down there fella!"

Sammy slipped below the sheets but only 10 seconds later he pops up and says "I'm sorry Agnes, I just can't do that, it really stinks down there"

"Awk thats just me Arthritis!" Agnes giggled.

"Arthritis doesn't smell" replied Sammy

"I know," says Agnes...... but I can't get my arm around to clean my arse!!!!!

Devastated

A very sad day today. After seven years of medical training and hard work, a very good friend of mine has been struck off after one minor indiscretion. He slept with one of his patients and can now no longer work in the profession. What a waste of time, effort, training and money. A genuinely nice guy and a brilliant vet...

Did you know that people in Dubai don't like the Flinstones?
But people in Abu Dhabi Dooooooooo

A pretty lady is standing on the side of a bridge, looking over it and thinking about jumping off. A homeless alcoholic man comes up to her as he was walking nearby. The lady notices the man coming and says: "Go away! There's nothing you can say to me to change my mind, you cannot help me." "Well, if you're going to kill yourself anyway, why don't we have sex? At least I'll enjoy it" replies the man. "No way, you're disgusting, go away." The homeless man turns and starts walking away. The lady thinks: "Is that all you were going to say to me? Nothing more? Won't you try to convince me that life is worth living that I should not jump off? Where are you going?" The homeless man thinks: "I have to make it down to the bottom. If I hurry, you'll still be warm."

I was in a cafe today and 2 waitresses had a massive row about how long to leave a teabag in a cup?
It got so bad that it ended in violence.
I asked the manager what happened and he said it had been brewing for ages.

Two owls playing pool when one owl who was attempting to pot a ball brushes another ball with his wing. The other owl says "ok that's two hits" the other owl says" two hits to who?"

For me golf is a lot like a woman - if she isn't holding my wood, she should be holding an iron.

I like jokes about eyes ... the cornea the better!

Fred the Texas farmer was in court with a claim against a lorry driver who crashed into him:
Lorry drivers attorney - "Fred at the scene you told the Highway Patrol

Officer you were and I quote "fine" and now you are here claiming for injuries totalling $100,000. Did you tell the Officer you were fine.
Farmer Fred - Well I was taking Daisy my favourite donkey.....
Attorney - "I'm sorry, you said you were fine is that not correct?"
Farmer Fred - Well I had just got Daisy loaded onto my truck and.....
Attorney -" Just answer with a yes or no please! Did you say you were fine?"
Farmer Fred - "Well I set off with Daisy to her favoutite field ....
Attorney -"Your Honour, can you please instruct the witness to answer with a simple yes or no answer!"
Judge - I'd like to hear the farmers side if you don't mind, carry on farmer Fred.
Farmer Fred - "Thank you your honour. Well as I got to the junction with the highway I stopped at the traffic lights and all of a sudden I was rear ended by a large lorry driven by that man. My truck was shoved over the highway and I was thrown into a ditch and poor Daisy was thrown into another one. "
Judge - "Go on."
Farmer Fred - "I was really sore and couldn't get up, I could hear Daisy making terrible noises and I just knew she was in a bad way. I tried to get up but I was too sore."
Attorney - "Your honour please!"
Judge - "No carry on farmer Fred"
Farmer Fred - " Poor Daisy was making such a din and I couldn't get over to help her and then this Highway Patrol Officer pulled up and walked over to Daisy I saw the look of horror on his face and then he pulled out his revolver and shot poor Daisy.
Judge - "my my that was a terrible thing he had to do"
Farmer fred - " Yes it was, but then he came over to me and asked, hey old fella, are you ok?" " Well what would you have said?"

My boss said to me, “You're the worst train driver ever. How many have you derailed this year?”
I said, “I'm not sure, it's hard to keep track.”

I've got a job as part of a human chess board. I'm on knights this week.

I hired a hitman to kill the wife.
He said, I'll shoot her just below the left nipple.
I replied, I want her dead, Not bloody kneecapped

My mate hired an eastern European as a cleaner, took her ten hours to do the hoovering.
Turns out she's a Slovak.

My housemates get mad with me when I steal their kitchen utensils!
But its a whisk i'm willing to take...

Woke up this morning and my Mrs wasn't in the house.
A note on the fridge said;
"Gone to live at my mums, this isn't working".
No idea what she was on about, the light came on when I opened the door and everything was still cold.

A good friend of mine was dyslexic.
He's dead now. He choked on his own vimto.

My clothes drying maiden has broken after years of fine service.
I'm gutted.
It's like the end of an airer.

My mate David is a victim of ID theft. Now we just call him 'Dav'

Lovemaking Tips For Seniors

1. Wear your glasses to make sure your partner is actually in the bed.
2. Set timer for 3 minutes, in case you doze off in the middle.
3. Set the mood with lighting. (Turn them ALL OFF!)
4. Make sure you put 999 on your speed dial before you begin.
5. Write partner's name on your hand in case you can't remember..
6. Use extra polygrip so your teeth don't end up under the bed.

7 Have Tylenol ready in case you actually complete the act..
8. Make all the noise you want....the neighbors are deaf, too.
9. If it works, call everyone you know with the good news!!
10. Don't even think about trying it twice.

The year is 2222 and Mike and Maureen land on Mars after accumulating enough frequent flier miles.
They meet a Martian couple and are talking about all sorts of things.
Mike asks if Mars has a stockmarket, if they have laptop computers, how they make money, etc.
Finally, Maureen brings up the subject of sex. "Just how do you guys do it ?" asks Maureen.
"Pretty much the way you do,"responds the Martian.
Discussion ensues and finally the couples decide to swap partners for the night and experience one another.
Maureen and the male Martian go off to a bedroom where the Martian strips.
He's got only a teeny, weeny member about half an inch long and just a quarter inch thick.
"I don't think this is going to work," says Maureen.
"Why?" he asks, "What's the matter?"
"Well," she replies, "It's just not long enough to reach me!"
"No problem," he says, and proceeds to slap his forehead with his palm.
With each slap of his forehead, his member grows until it's quite impressively long.
"Well," she says, "That's quite impressive, but it's still pretty narrow...."
"No problem," he says, and starts pulling his ears.
With each pull,his member grows wider and wider until the entire measurement is extremely exciting to the woman.
"Wow!" she exclaims, as they fell into bed and made mad, passionate love.

The next day the couples rejoin their normal partners and go their separate ways.
As they walk along, Mike asks "Well, was it any good?"
"I hate to say it," says Maureen, "but it was pretty wonderful. How about you ?"
"It was horrible," he replies.
"All I got was a headache. All she kept doing the whole time was slapping my forehead and pulling my ears."

I bought my nephew a fridge for his birthday.
Maybe not the most exciting present for a seven-year-old, but you should have seen his face light up when he opened it.

A juggernaut full of onions has shed its load all over the M1.
Motorists are advised to find a hard shoulder to cry on.

Venison for dinner again? Oh deer!
How does Moses make tea? Hebrews it.
England has no kidney bank, but it does have a Liverpool.
I tried to catch some fog, but I mist.
They told me I had type-A blood, but it was a typo.
I changed my iPod's name to Titanic. It's syncing now.
Jokes about German sausage are the wurst.
I stayed up all night to see where the sun went, and then it dawned on

me.
When chemists die, they barium.
Why were the Indians here first? They had reservations.
I didn't like my beard at first. Then it grew on me.
Did you hear about the cross-eyed teacher who lost her job
because she couldn't control her pupils?
When you get a bladder infection, urine trouble.
Broken pencils are pointless.
What do you call a dinosaur with an extensive vocabulary? A thesaurus.
I dropped out of communism class because of lousy Marx.
I got a job at a bakery because I kneaded dough.
Velcro - what a rip off!

It's amazing how some key inventions come as a result of simple incidents. Cats eyes in the road were invented when a guy was driving down the road in the pitch black and saw a cat walking towards him. The cats eyes reflected his headlights and 'cats eyes' in the road were born. If the cat had been walking in the opposite direction he might have invented the pencil sharpener.

'OLD' IS WHEN...
Your sweetie says, 'Let's go upstairs and make love,' and you answer, 'Pick one; I can't do both!'
Your friends compliment you on your new alligator shoes and you're barefoot.
Going bra-less pulls all the wrinkles out of your face
you don't care where your spouse goes, just as long as you don't have to

go along.
You are cautioned to slow down by the doctor instead of by the police.
'Getting a little action' means you don't need to take a laxative today.
'Getting lucky' means you find your car in the parking lot.
An 'all-nighter' means not getting up to use the bathroom.
You're not sure if these are facts or jokes!!

I was a very happy man. My wonderful Italian girlfriend and I had been dating for over a year. So we decided to get married.
There was only one little thing bothering me.
It was her beautiful younger sister, Sofia.
My prospective sister-in-law was twenty-two, wore very tight miniskirts, and generally was bra-less.
She would regularly bend down when she was near me. I always got more than a nice view.
It had to be deliberate. She never did it around anyone else.
One day she called me and asked me to come over. 'To check my Sister's wedding- invitations' she said.
She was alone when I arrived. She whispered to me that she had feelings and desires for me. She couldn't overcome them anymore.
She told me that she wanted me just once before I got married. She said "Before you commit your life to my sister".

Well, I was in total shock, and I couldn't say a word. She said, "I'm going upstairs to my bedroom" she said, "if you want one last wild fling, just come up and have me".
I was stunned and frozen in shock as I watched her go up the stairs.
I stood there for a moment. Then turned and made a bee-line straight to the front door. I opened the door, and headed straight towards my car.
Lo and behold, my entire future family was standing outside, all clapping!
With tears in his eyes, my future father-in-law hugged me. He said, 'My

son, we are very happy that you have passed our little test. We couldn't ask for a better man for our daughter. Welcome to the family my son.'
And the moral of this story is:
Always keep your condoms in your car!!

I was in the kitchen earlier when a flying insect came in through the open window and then suddenly exploded.
I think it was a jihaddy longlegs?

I put a bet on a horse this afternoon called Frozen Tap....... It didn't run!

I phoned up Gamblers Anonymous today at 12.00p.m.
They said they were really busy and asked me to ring back at 20 to 1.

We've got an aviary at home, but one of our birds of prey will only exercise at night to the sounds of '80s synth pop. Our kestrel manoeuvres in the dark.

Paddy's pregnant sister is involved in a terrible car accident and ends up in a coma.
After being in the coma for nearly six months, she wakes and discovers she is no longer pregnant. So she asks the doctor about her baby.

The doctor replies “Ma’am you had twins! A boy and a girl. The babies are fine now but they were very poorly at birth and had to christen them immediately - your brother named them."
The woman says " Suffering Jesus no, not me brother, he's ******* clueless!"
So expecting the worse she asks the doctor what are their names
The doctor says” Well your daughter is Denise" the woman says” Denise, that's a fine name, I guess I was wrong about me brother."
" What's the boy's name?" she asks
To which the doctor replies
" DENEPHEW!"

A lady bodybuilder went to see her GP to discuss a particular situation she was faced with.
The Doctor asked "What appears to be the problem then?"
She said "Well I've grown a penis since I started taking steroids!"
The Doctor continued "Anabolic?"
She replied "No, just the penis".

Two guys went to a petrol station that was holding a contest: a chance to win free sex when you filled your tank. They pumped their petrol and went to pay the male attendant.
"I'm thinking of a number between one and ten," he said. "If you guess right, you win free sex."
"Okay," agreed one of the guys, "I guess seven."
"Sorry, I was thinking of eight," replied the attendant.
The next week they tried again. When they went to pay, the attendant told them to pick a number.

"Two!" said the second guy.
"Sorry, it's three, said the attendant. "Come back and try again."
As they walked out to their car, one guy said to the other, "I think this contest is rigged."
"No way," said his buddy. "My wife won twice last week."

A Texan decided to write a book about famous churches around the world, so he bought a plane ticket and took a trip to Rome. On his first day he was inside a church taking photographs when he noticed a golden telephone mounted on the wall with a sign that read $10,000 per call
The American, being intrigued, asked a priest who was strolling by, what the telephone was used for. The priest replied that it was a direct line to Heaven and that for $10,000 you could talk to God. The American thanked the priest and went along his way.
His next stop was in Moscow. There, at a very large cathedral, he saw the same golden telephone with the same sign under it. He wondered if this was the same kind of telephone he saw in Rome and he asked a nun what its purpose was. She told him that it was a direct line to Heaven and that for $10,000 he could talk to God. "OK. Thank you," said the American.
He then travelled to France, Israel, Germany and Brazil. In every church he saw the same golden telephone with a "$10,000 per call" sign under it.
The American finally decided to travel to Scotland to see if the Scots had the same telephone. He arrived in Glasgow and again, in Glasgow Cathedral, there was the same golden telephone, but this time the sign under it read "20p per call". The American was surprised so he asked the minister about the sign. "Minister, I've travelled all over the world and I've seen this same golden telephone in many churches. I'm told that it is a direct line to heaven, but everywhere I went the price was $10,000 per call. Why is it so cheap here?"

The minister smiled and answered, "You're in Scotland now son. It's a local call."

The lead singer of Chumbawumba is married to a champion breakdancer. She had to give up dancing when she fell pregnant, but only three months after giving birth she successfully defended her world title!
She got knocked up, but she got down again...

Saw some snooty fellow taking a fish for a stroll this morning.
Was walking around like he owned the plaice.

A teacher at a school for obese children was sacked recently for taking Ecstasy during playtime
His massive pupils gave him away

I must be ill - I thought I saw a sausage fly past my window, but it was actually a seabird.
I think I've taken a tern for the wurst

I've just to the bakers & I said to the baker " how come all your cakes are 50p but that one over there is a £1 "
He said that's Madeira cake.

I wasn't very close to my gran when she died,
good job really she was hit by a bus.

How do you catch a unique rabbit? You unique up on him.
How do you catch a tame rabbit? The tame way!

Police have confirmed a man has been arrested in Burnley after falling into a combine harvester whilst trying to steal it.
He is due to be bailed tomorrow...

There's a bloke on here called Buster, who keeps sending me loads & loads of video links of the 1970's glam rock group, The Sweet.
Does anyone know a way, there's got to be a way,
To block Buster!

"Conjunctivitis.com – that's a site for sore eyes"

"I have kleptomania, but when it gets bad, I take something for it."

"I want to die like my father, peacefully in his sleep, not screaming and terrified, like his passengers."

"I was mugged by a man on crutches, wearing camouflage. Ha ha, I thought, you can hide but you can't run."

"How come Miss Universe is only ever won by people from Earth?"

"I saw a pair of knickers today – on the front it said, 'I would do anything for love' and on the back it said 'but I won't do that.'"

A German tourist jumped in the river and saved a dog from drowning.Upon getting back up on the bridge he checked the dog out and told the owner that"zer dog iss ok,und vill be fine"She asked if he was a vet?He replied,"Vet? I'm facking soaking!"

I've had to close my chicken dating agency due to financial problems.
I was struggling to make hens meet.